ESTHER
A Channel of Grace

ESTHER

A Channel of Grace

A NOVEL BY
Patience Satoro

Esther: A Channel of Grace
Published by Patience Satoro
with Castle Publishing Ltd
New Zealand

© 2023 Patience Satoro

ISBN 978-0-473-65717-8 (Softcover)
ISBN 978-0-473-65718-5 (ePUB)
ISBN 978-0-473-65719-2 (Kindle)

Editing:
Laura Edge, Daphne Stringer
and Sally Webster

Production & Typesetting:
Andrew Killick
Castle Publishing Services
www.castlepublishing.co.nz

Cover Design:
Paul Smith

The names and storyline are inspired by
the book of Esther as found in the Bible.

Contents

1

THE PALACE

KING XERXES STOOD ON the balcony and gazed out at the scene that lay before him. His focus was momentarily distracted by an eagle that suddenly came into view and circled the skies just above the palace. It was interesting to watch as it glided effortlessly under the jet-blue sky; it might have been looking for prey as it drifted towards the surrounding mountains. His gaze panned back and settled on the lush beauty of the gardens; they were at their best at this time of the year, and he admired the vibrant splashes of colour. Sprawling green lawns merged into shrubs and larger bushes, which in turn gradually blended into the forest which nestled at the foot of the gently-sloping mountains that wrapped around his kingdom. It was as though he was looking at a beautiful painting – shades of green adorned with vivid splashes of colour from the artist's brush.

Xerxes inhaled deeply, enjoying the lovely scent wafting on the morning breeze. A sweet aroma came from the many rose bushes spread across the garden. Such beauty would instil a sense of peace and calm in anyone, and it seemed to have that effect on the king. Dressed in a rather casual way, he stood motionless; the only movement came from his long, grey linen gown, which fluttered in the gentle wind. It was beautifully embroidered in an ornate design, and had a thread that matched his loose-fitting linen pants.

Before Xerxes had ascended the throne, the palace could have been described as being cold and distant; it had exuded a sullen sombreness that made one imagine it was haunted. He had suffered many a chill before determining to transform it into a space that was regal, warm and welcoming. At the start of his tenure the palace staff had matched the palace's cold and sombre demeanour; they behaved in a rigid and stoic manner, living in constant fear of being called out for doing one thing or another. Xerxes easily understood why – his predecessor had been a drill-sergeant type of king who had demanded his orders be obeyed, and who had been known to order an execution over a burnt steak! His behaviour had been epitomised by dramatic outbursts, followed by serious consequences of various kinds.

King Xerxes had gradually and painstakingly transformed the interiors of the palace so that they were now warmer and more welcoming. The chilling silence that once lingered in the corridors was now replaced with the sound of soft chit-chat as the staff went about their work. They had slowly adapted to the warm demeanour that the new king had brought with him, and now they loved being in the palace.

Equally pleasing was the transformation of the vast lawn which had served as the palace garden. The gardening team had been dispatched on expeditions far and wide in search of trees, bushes, plants and flowers to create the garden the king desired. King Xerxes had worked closely with the head gardener in designing a stunning new landscape that bore no resemblance to the original at all. The result was astounding, to say the least. Although the new park-like grounds were huge, the king had made good use of every bit of space. The addition of rockeries and pathways helped make it look like a piece of paradise. The pond that had once looked bleak was now picturesque and brimming with life, and was a perfect finish to the corner of the garden that could easily have been voted as the best section of all.

Xerxes had ordered another corner to be partitioned off as an enclosed indoor area where events could be hosted. The staff were still at pains to understand how he had dreamed it up, the first of its kind in the kingdom, and the end result had blown their minds.

Xerxes had also designated areas of the palace as special places he could retreat to whenever he needed time out. Unlike previous kings, who had constantly demanded their servants be close by in order to be able to respond to their every beck and call, Xerxes often preferred spending time in private spaces, where he could withdraw and be alone without interruption.

The king had ordered that the dusty stonework of the bleak balcony outside his chambers be scrubbed and polished. The once pale and faded granite stones were now a deep, shiny grey, and smooth to the touch. He had large flowerpots filled with exotic shrubs placed around the balcony; the croton plants he had ordered from the adjoining kingdom were soon flourishing and added vibrant colour to this newly-renovated space.

Xerxes found the balcony therapeutic. He came here early in the day when he needed to energise and focus, and later on when he wanted to clear his mind and unwind after a long day's work. This was *his* space, and no one else had direct access to this part of the palace; the only way to it was through his chambers. He had requested that a swing chair with a canopy be set in the corner, close to the edge. From this chair he had a sweeping view of the gardens and the rugged mountain range that surrounded his kingdom. He viewed these mountains as a protective wall, hemming it in and shielding it from attack. Unbeknownst to many, these mountains hid watchmen who were constantly on the lookout for suspicious activity. They worked around the clock in shifts so that there were men on the lookout for enemy invasion at all times. King Xerxes had a deep love for his kingdom, and he took pains to ensure that peace prevailed at all costs.

To the left of the gardens were the stables and paddocks. These were subdivided to cater for the many different breeds that the king had managed to acquire over the years. Most of the horses had been gifted to him by the leaders of the different provinces in his kingdom. The paddock closest to the king's balcony was home to an incredibly special horse which he had befittingly named Pegasus. It was easy to understand why he held Pegasus so close to his heart, loving it more than the others. The horse had been gifted to him as a colt by an empress from a far-off kingdom. His coat was pure white and appeared to shimmer in the sun, and his mane fell effortlessly in waves on both sides of his neck, giving him the appearance of a fairy horse. Grooming Pegasus required little effort, and a simple brush down seemed to make him glow all the more. He would canter to meet the king when he saw him standing at the paddock fence, and even allowed Xerxes to run his hands through his mane. There was a strong bond between this majestic creature and his master, but this had not been built overnight; Xerxes had had to use all manner of tricks to gain his trust.

On an ordinary day, King Xerxes would have settled into his chair to unwind and take in the beauty spread before his eyes, but on this occasion he did not feel like sitting down at all. Instead he leaned on the balcony wall, his bare arms feeling the coldness of the hard granite against his warm skin. This sent a small chill up his arm and caused him to shiver involuntarily. His eyes roamed from the majestic horse in the paddock to the large pond at the bottom of the garden. A mischievous smile quivered on his lips. *I wonder what my household would think if I were to go down there for a swim?* he wondered. He had never done that before, but the thought often crossed his mind when he stood on the balcony. Many would have found it hard to imagine that the king had a hidden sense of humour.

King Xerxes' reign was far reaching, stretching from Cush to India, and he ruled over one hundred and twenty-seven provinces.

His throne sat in the citadel of Susa. On the outside he exuded great power and command, but on the inside he had a great sense of humour, mixed with gentleness, warmth and love. Few people knew this softer side of him. But if they had paid close attention they might have noticed his softly creased eyes, which twinkled whenever he was in a playful mood. But because he was king, Xerxes had successfully built a wall of steel around his emotions, rarely letting his guard down.

Over the past six months Xerxes had been on a kingdom tour to inspect the glory and vastness of his kingdom. He had used it as a means of highlighting the power and extent of his reign to the nobles and dignitaries in the different provinces, and to instil an appreciation of kingdom matters in those he had chosen for leadership positions. On top of that, he had seen it as a way of strengthening loyalty and ensuring that leaders would side with him should any threat arise.

The highlight of this tour was to be a banquet at the palace that would last for seven days – one that would not only mark the end of his tour but also provide an opportunity for the dignitaries to strengthen their relationships. All of the princes, nobles, officials and military leaders of Persia and Media had been invited. And not only them – Xerxes planned opening the banquet to everyone in the citadel of Susa, from the least to the greatest. It was to be a period of feasting and drinking, with a plentiful supply of the finest wines from the palace vineyards.

The day of the much-awaited celebratory banquet was fast approaching. From his balcony King Xerxes could see into the enclosed garden where the festivities would take place. And it seemed that the preparations were progressing well. He trusted that all of his orders had been successfully implemented; he did not want anything omitted. He had every confidence in his banqueting manager – a stout man of vast experience who oversaw all the events that took place at the palace. He had requested that each day a different province be showcased, and had spent weeks with his team instructing them in detail as to what he desired. They knew that his guests were to be pampered and left free to network.

As he thought about the complexity of the arrangements, a knot of anxiety formed in the pit of his stomach. But, as he continued gazing at the breath-taking view of the gardens, he calmed down. He then noticed the basket-shaped bamboo chair tucked away in a corner, and he went over and eased himself into it. It was big enough to seat two people, and was filled with soft, light-green cushions. Attached to a metal frame by two chains, it swung freely back and forth. Several matching bamboo tables were located strategically around the balcony, giving the area an exotic look.

As he sank into the soft green cushions, Xerxes felt a sense of relief to be off his feet, and his hand automatically reached for the bowl of fruit on the table beside him. He chose his favourite treat – juicy, green grapes, freshly picked from the vine. He pulled them from the bunch one by one and, chewing them slowly, savoured their sweetness. From the comfort of his chair he could see a different aspect of the garden – the section his wife Queen Vashti loved and spent most of her time in.

Xerxes admired his wife, and he found it amusing that she loved flowers so much. She loved showing them off to her visitors, and enjoyed creating her own floral arrangements on special occasions. In fact, Vashti loved all things beautiful.

I wonder what helter-skelter arrangements are being made as she co-ordinates her banquet? he mused. For, while the men were having their seven days of banqueting, the women would be enjoying their own festivities – hosted by Queen Vashti herself. Her posture now, as she picked fresh flowers for the dinner tables, said it all. He could see that while she was picking them almost mechanically her mind was ticking away, no doubt for the umpteenth time trying to refine her plans. He silently hoped that the week-long event would not take its toll on her health.

As he watched her his mind drifted back to when they had met, and how captivated he had been, and still was, by her. Her unsurpassed beauty still made him catch his breath every time she walked into a room. She was well-practised in making grand entrances, and revelled in the attention she received as his queen. Vashti's eyes always captivated him; whenever he was depleted and needed recharging, simply looking into their mysterious green depths made him feel instantly refreshed. She was without doubt his greatest source of inspiration. Her high cheekbones, full lips and even teeth accentuated her engaging smile. Xerxes considered his wife to be the most beautiful woman to walk the earth, and he could not imagine himself with any other. Watching her pick flowers in the garden, he was as captivated by her now as he had been when he had first set eyes on her.

Vashti must have sensed his presence, for she turned her gaze in his direction. Though the distance between them was great, he felt her eyes linger on him. They shared a bond that was unusually strong; it was unimaginable that anyone or anything could ever break it. Xerxes lifted his hand and waved to her, and she blew back a playful kiss. He mimicked a catch, placing it on his chest. The echo of her laughter was music to his ears. She was the only person who was privy to the king's playful nature.

The King lingered a little longer on the balcony; he was putting off tackling the many responsibilities that awaited him. He would have to force himself away from this little piece of paradise in order to check on the progress of banquet preparations. He had strategically allocated the enclosed garden for his banquet, and had generously allowed Queen Vashti to use the banqueting hall in the royal palace for hers. This arrangement was not entirely selfish, for he knew Vashti would enjoy showing the immense beauty of the palace to her guests, and this would not have been possible had he allocated her one of the other enclosed gardens. The ladies were bound to appreciate the fine art and precious ornaments that were housed in the palace; he doubted his male guests would notice any of it.

The king thought about the wine for the banquet, and immediately took a turn to the wine cellar. Few people were permitted access to this section of the palace, and he was confident he would not meet anyone on his way there, especially at this time of the day. The life of a king is usually short on privacy; on most occasions an aide would have been tailing him. He had, however, managed this problem by requesting that aides stay away from the north-facing wing. He smiled to himself in gratitude, wondering which king had ruled against servants being allowed into the royal wine cellar; he valued having this place all to himself, and agreed: *great minds think alike.*

Xerxes approached the stairway with caution as it was steep, small and narrow, and appeared to have been hewn from a rock. His long legs could have taken in two steps at a time, but he was in no rush. He wanted to enjoy each moment, so he patiently took them one by one. The temperature seemed to drop with each step, bringing him closer to the majestic door that shut off the cool cellar from the outside world. The door itself was not an ordinary door – it had intricate vines, huge bunches of grapes and wine goblets carved onto it. The wine cellar had been created before his time, and he smiled in amusement as he wondered whether it had been his father, grandfather or maybe his great-grandfather who had ordered the decorative artwork. Whoever it was, he could sense that they had been passionate about artistic expression. A smile of appreciation lingered on his lips as he tried to envision the dedication, time and hard work that had gone into designing this elaborate cellar door. It was indeed a fine work of art.

The king lifted up the heavy gold-plated knocker, letting it swing back down with a loud, resounding *bang*. Such a sound was difficult to miss, and he did not expect to have to repeat it. Within seconds the king heard the wine steward shuffle to the door and fumble with the locks. It swung slowly open; this could not have been executed any faster because it was so heavy. The wine steward had a look of irritation on his face. *Who could this be?* It was not often that he got visitors to his world of wines. The irritation was immediately replaced with a beaming smile when he realised that his unexpected visitor was in fact the king himself!

'Your Majesty,' he said bowing deeply, clearly alarmed to receive a royal visit. 'What a pleasure and honour it is to see you. Please do come in! How may I serve you, Your Majesty?' His eyes instinctively inspected the cellar before he slowly shut the door behind them. Outwardly he was calm, but his heart was doing a wild dance inside his chest, panicking about what could possibly have caused the king to come down to his cellar. He was more accustomed to receiving instructions via messengers; to have the king himself appear was a rare occurrence indeed!

Xerxes perceived the wine steward's nervousness and tried to put him at ease. He was used to this reaction from some of his staff, so he came right to the point.

'I've come down to check on how you are doing with the wine for the banquet,' he said.

'It is coming along well, my great and mighty king,' responded the steward with new confidence. 'Would you like a taste, Your Majesty?' Then without waiting for a response, he pulled a golden goblet from the cabinet and poured some wine, fresh from the barrel, for the king. Xerxes accepted the wine with a brief nod, lifted it to his nose and inhaled slowly, and finally took a small sip. He swirled it around in his mouth, appreciating the complex flavours, before swallowing.

'Mmm, very promising,' he commented.

'Thank you, Your Majesty. The grapes are of exquisite quality, and a delight to work with,' the wine steward responded.

Xerxes then proceeded to where the barrels for the banquet had been placed. There were a large number of them there, and the pungent, woody aroma suggested it was wine that had progressed well in maturity.

'Our guests are in for a special treat,' commented Xerxes, more to himself than anyone else. He continued to stroll around the cellar for a while longer, stopping at times to ask questions, all the while sipping the wine in his goblet. It tasted smooth, and he was confident its rich flavour would more than satisfy his guests. The wine steward followed at a respectful distance, waiting for any suggestions that might come his way. The king eventually handed back an empty goblet.

'This wine is maturing well,' he said. 'You have done an excellent job; well done!' This compliment was received with a wide smile from the steward.

'Thank you, Your Majesty. I will not disappoint you.'

Xerxes was well pleased with his surprise visit to the cellar, and felt prepared for what the rest of the day would hold. As the huge cellar door closed behind him, he ascended the steep steps with renewed dedication to face the other business of the day.

2

THE PARTY

THE BANQUET WAS IN full swing and the atmosphere was merry. King Xerxes sat on an elevated seat specially created for the occasion, and from this he had a full view of the entire area. The servants had clearly gone to great lengths to carry out his instructions to the finest detail. They had outdone themselves, and he was satisfied.

The garden was adorned with hangings of blue and white linen, made specially for the occasion, and they brought a cool freshness to the atmosphere. The marble columns were adorned with decorations, and the pavement, made of porphyry, marble, mother-of-pearl and other precious stones, glistened from the rigorous polishing it had received. Couches covered in gold and silver drapes were placed strategically around the enclosed garden; they were now occupied by guests, deep in conversation. Xerxes had been unsure whether to include the couches, and was pleased to observe his guests now making good use of them.

Tables had been arranged towards the back of the enclosed garden, with ample space between the guests' ones and those of the king. The layout was designed to give people adequate space to move about freely. Garlands of fresh flowers had been fixed between short poles surrounding the entire area, adding their sweet perfume to the occasion. The servants were kept busy filling and refilling the guests' cups with wine, and a band of musicians played merry tunes in the background. Everyone was in high spirits, and a mixture of lively chatter and laughter resounded in this uniquely-enclosed space. As he sat back in his luxurious chair, the smile on Xerxes' face displayed his satisfaction at the success of both his campaign and these festivities.

For the past seven days, different groups of people, both high and low, and from all over the kingdom, had come through the doors. Xerxes was well pleased with the high turnout and keen interest in attending the event, the first of its kind in the kingdom. He felt it would prove pivotal in his being able to work more closely with his leaders, and in cementing their loyalty. He strolled around, ensuring that he met with everyone. Security was tight throughout the week, as was fitting for an occasion involving the king and countless dignitaries of such high stature. Despite the freely-flowing goodwill, Xerxes was aware that anything unexpected could happen. His guards had taken precautions to ensure that security was tight, and that history would not repeat itself. A shudder went down his spine as he recalled the cold-blooded assassination of one of his uncles.

On a more cheerful note, Xerxes was delighted that the chefs had outdone themselves in providing an astonishing array of foods from all of the regions in his kingdom. Drawn from the various provinces, each one had done a sterling job in providing unique and tantalising flavours for the king and his guests. No two meals were the same; the varied menu was the highlight of the banquet. Guests ate to their hearts' content, eagerly trying new delicacies. King Xerxes made a silent vow to travel more widely in the future, realising that he still had much to explore in the great diversity of his kingdom.

The guest turnout was slightly larger than the king had anticipated. Barrel after barrel full of cool wine had been hoisted up from the cellar, decanted and then rolled back again. So great was the revelling guests' thirst, he dared not enquire whether the stock was going to hold out. Mercifully, it did. Indeed, on the last day it was evident that the king himself had partaken a little too freely of it – and this usually meant that something interesting was about to happen!

The king was, by this stage, in high spirits, along with everyone else, and giddy with happiness. He felt elated that his chosen venue had catered so well for the crowd, and eminently satisfied that everyone seemed to be enjoying themselves so much. Carried away with the excitement of the party, he wondered what he could do to make the evening extra special and somehow even more memorable for his guests. His eyes searched to and fro as he pondered, eventually coming to rest on a huge portrait of Queen Vashti that hung on a wall of the garden. A brilliant idea immediately formed in his wine-spiced mind, and his eyes began to twinkle. Without any hesitation he scanned the room for servants to carry out his spur-of-the-moment plan; he had decided to give his guests the rare opportunity of meeting their queen in person!

Xerxes had concluded that it would not be right for the banquet to end and his guests to return to their provinces without having been introduced to Queen Vashti. He wanted to show off his beautiful wife, the pride of his life. He could not foresee any problems with this brilliant idea. His face lit up with pride as he pictured her floating like an angel around the room filled with dignitaries. Without a second thought, he signalled to his seven eunuchs. They seemed to move around together in a cluster; if one was spotted, the others would not be far away. Their duty was to linger close to the king and be ready to carry out his wishes at all times.

'Go and approach the queen,' he told them. 'Request that she grace my banquet with her presence.' He provided no further details, but his instructions were clear. They scurried out, leaving the king with his face shining with expectation and beaming from ear to ear with excitement as he waited for the dramatic entrance of his wife.

Word that the king had requested that the queen come and grace their banquet spread quickly, and the guests were elated as they waited for her arrival. For some, this would be the first time they had been in the same room as her, and they envisioned themselves bowing deeply or shaking her soft hand; others formed eloquent greetings in their minds. Gradually they settled down and returned to their merry-making, knowing that there was quite some distance between the garden and the royal palace where Queen Vashti was entertaining the women. Expecting that she would perhaps take some time to ready herself for the glamorous entrance, they prepared to wait patiently.

Meanwhile the seven eunuchs – Mehuman, Biztha, Harbona, Bigtha, Abagtha, Zethar and Karcas – left the enclosed garden with their heads held high. They knew that the king would only send his most trusted servants on such an important mission. This would be their shining moment, as all the guests would see just how important they were. Each wondered which two of them would be chosen to walk in beside the queen. Excitement bubbled inside them as they envisioned marching back and announcing, 'Queen Vashti!'

<u>3</u>

THE DEFIANT QUEEN

THE MOOD IN THE royal palace, where the ladies were gathered, was every bit as festive as the king's celebrations. Queen Vashti was elated that her banquet had turned out just as she had envisioned. Sitting in an elevated chair, her hair was loosely pinned on the top of her head, a few wavy strands cascading down each side of her face. This style was elegant, and made her appear even taller. Queen Vashti was an excellent hostess, always presenting a dazzling smile and speaking in a gentle voice, which gave her an air of sophistication and mystery.

The queen's guests were mesmerised by her. They were all having the time of their lives, exquisitely dressed in fine gowns of every design and colour. Each lady had gone to great lengths to look her best; the seamstresses throughout the kingdom had been kept very busy in the weeks prior to this event. The result was a banqueting hall of beautiful women having a wonderful time together. They adored their queen, and felt privileged to have been invited. Like the king, they held Vashti in very high esteem. Some had come to admire her beauty, whilst others were content with simply hearing her voice.

There was no one as beautiful as Vashti in the banqueting hall. Her face glowed, and her eyes sparkled with a deep sense of satisfaction at how her event was turning out. On this last day of the banquet she wore an intricately-detailed turquoise gown which swept the floor as she glided gracefully across the hall. Underneath the layers of rich fabric, her feet were enveloped in delicate silver slippers that had been designed especially for her.

The banqueting hall decor was perfect, the linen drapes setting off the huge vases of roses that were placed at different stations around the perimeter. The couches scattered around the room had elaborately-dressed ladies with wine goblets reclining on them and chatting away in excitement. The musicians were playing a merry tune, and some of the women were enjoying dancing to the music. The atmosphere was one of carefree pleasure and celebration.

Vashti loved being queen. She adored her husband the king, a quick smile gently flickering on her lips as thoughts of him played in her mind. She knew full well that the honour and power of her position came through him alone. She did not have to raise her voice whenever she needed anything done – everyone fell over themselves to fulfil her every need. She could not envisage herself apart from this life and the benefits it afforded her; she loved everything about it.

The banquet was still in full swing when Vashti's roving eyes picked up the procession of eunuchs heading towards the palace. Being in command in her own domain, she was alert to anything unusual in her vicinity. She wondered what they wanted, as she and the king had agreed that the two parties would be kept separate. An uninvited feeling of defensiveness arose inside of her. This part of the palace was designated for the ladies, and she did not want anyone or anything to disrupt her banquet. She became more and more perturbed as she watched the procession arrive at the entrance hall, where they halted and spoke to one of her royal maidservants. It took some time for them to deliver their message, but eventually the maidservant made her way to Vashti, who was by now very curious about it all.

'Please excuse me for a moment,' the queen said, indicating to the women who had come to greet her that she needed to receive the coming message in private. 'I need to take care of some business. But I will send for you as soon as I can.'

'King Xerxes requests your presence at the king's banquet,' the maidservant said on approaching the queen.

'Is that so?' responded Vashti, quite taken aback by this request and trying not to show it.

'The eunuchs will walk you to the men's banquet as soon as you are ready,' confidently added the maid.

The change in Vashti's demeanour was subtle and might not have been noticed, but there was an immediate check in her mood as she considered this request. She believed she could read the king's intentions like a book. He was aware she enjoyed attention, and a ripple of excitement ran through her body as she envisioned herself gliding into the enclosed garden along with her chosen entourage. Then almost immediately a twinge of apprehension at the king's impromptu request then tugged within her.

The sight of the eunuchs standing pretentiously in the entrance-way quickly smothered the last small flame of excitement which had momentarily lit up inside her. She felt inconvenienced by this spontaneous summons. Something about the way they stood waiting impatiently caused a rush of stubborn defiance to rise within her. So the king expected her to abandon her own guests, drop everything at such short notice and rush over to him! In a split second she resolved that no one, not even the king, should be permitted to order her around on a whim. And without further thought or consultation, she decided she would *not* make an appearance at the king's banquet that night.

Vashti's maidservant was waiting for a reply. The queen beckoned to her and whispered something in her ear. The maid's expression quickly changed from one of expectation to one of disbelief, and then a cold dread at being the bearer of this news. The queen's response was an ice-cold rejection of the summons.

'Advise the eunuchs that I will not be joining the king at his banquet as I cannot excuse myself from my own,' ordered Vashti. The maid had turned pale as she considered how she was going to convey this negative response to the waiting eunuchs.

'I will finish my banquet on a high note,' continued the queen, 'and will not leave my guests unattended at any time.' The queen's defiant spirit made her confident, and she failed to consider any error in her decision. She had never defied the king before, and was therefore unaware of the consequences of such an act.

The royal maidservant was stunned at the queen's refusal of the king; however, she recognised the look that the queen got on her face when she had made her mind up about a matter, and she knew it was no use trying to reason with her. With heavy steps she crossed the hall to the eunuchs.

'I relayed your request exactly as you told me,' she explained to the waiting eunuchs. 'I told the queen that the king had requested her presence at his banquet.'

'Yes, that was the request,' they responded in unison.

'Well, when will she be coming out?' asked Harbona with a hint of impatience.

'Queen Vashti has advised that she will not be coming,' the maid replied in a rush, her eyes closed.

'She said she is not coming?' echoed the eunuchs in disbelief.

'Yes, that is correct,' responded the maidservant. 'The queen has stated that she cannot excuse herself from her own banquet at such short notice.'

The eunuchs were dumbfounded. Their instincts told them that this was not going to end well. 'We will go in and speak with her,' declared Harbona. It was evident that they were not convinced that the maid had relayed their message clearly enough. 'Please lead us to where she is!' he instructed. 'Bigtha, come with me.'

The two senior eunuchs immediately entered the banquet hall to deliver the request to the queen face to face. They were intent on succeeding in their mission.

Queen Vashti was back in her elevated seat and busy chatting with a fresh group of ladies, trying her nest to give them her full attention. Her flowing turquoise gown was draped around her in a cloud-like manner, creating a perfect setting for her beauty. As she caught sight of the two approaching, a renewed surge of defiance welled up inside her. The queen resolved that nothing and nobody would make her change her mind about going to the king's banquet. Her eyes became cold as she prepared to receive them.

The ladies sitting closest to the queen were uncertain about whether they should leave or stay. They sipped their drinks nervously and averted their eyes from the approaching eunuchs; these men were high-level, well-respected officials in the kingdom, and it was well known how closely they worked with the king.

'I just need to take care of a small matter. Will you please excuse me?' The group of ladies, quite relieved, quickly left the presence of Vashti as they sensed that she needed to discuss an important matter with the approaching eunuchs.

The eunuchs bowed in respect before Vashti; they held her in high esteem and greeted her humbly.

'Your Majesty, the king requests your presence at the men's banquet,' declared Harbona. 'Please would you be kind enough to reconsider your decision and come with us?'

'Please convey my apologies to the king. This is the last day of my banquet, and it would be most unbecoming of me to leave my guests unattended,' the queen responded in a firm tone. 'I trust that he will understand my position,' she added, flashing the duo one of her sweetest smiles.

'If you would reconsider, we could ensure your swift return to your guests,' ventured Bigtha in an attempt to reason with her. But she refused to be swayed in her decision.

Despite their best attempts to persuade her, Vashti remained unmoved, reiterating that she would not leave her guests, and all the while maintaining a most gracious smile on her face. They tried as much as they dared to press the queen into accompanying them; however, it had become clear to them that she was not going to change her mind, and they were left with no option but to bow deeply and return to the king with the news that she had refused. Their heads now hung low in a mixture of disgrace and consternation. *How was the king was going to react to such defiance?* They took their time as they retraced their steps back to his banquet, delaying the inevitable humiliation that Vashti's response would bring on him.

The queen experienced a sudden feeling of unease as the eunuchs took their leave of her. There was a nagging whisper in her spirit telling her to reconsider her decision and appear at the king's banquet as he had requested. However, she ignored this soft inner voice, and then totally silenced it by sending for the ladies she had just dismissed and resuming conversation. She kept justifying her decision by telling herself, *I am the host of the ladies' party, and should not have to leave my guests unattended.*

However, soon the feeling of alarm started to build up again, but it was now far too late to reconsider, as the eunuchs had already left for the king's banquet. She tried to convince herself that it was the wine that had caused the king to summon her; she was sure he would overlook the whole matter as soon as the banquet was over and he had sobered up. She stood up from her elevated seat and went around the hall, much to the delight of her guests. She paid extra attention to all her guests and none detected the turmoil raging inside of her. Try as she might, she could not shake off the uneasy feeling that simmered in the pit of her stomach. She vacillated between thinking that everything was going to be all right and being upset about defying the king. Outwardly she kept a smile on her face, putting on a convincing front so that her guests would not notice the change in her. Eventually she felt a pang of sadness, as she realised how disappointed the king would be. *I will make it up to you, my love*, she resolved.

The eunuchs were now in uncharted territory, and wondered how they were going to break the news of the queen's unprecedented refusal to the king. She had defied the command, his golden sceptre raised towards her, summoning her to approach his throne. Mehuman and Biztha entered the garden to deliver the devastating news, while the other five remained outside. It was the longest walk of shame the two had ever had to take, as they walked from the entrance of the enclosed garden towards the throne. The king and his guests were waiting in anticipation for Queen Vashti to appear.

Upon instruction from the king, an extra couch had been made ready in anticipation of her arrival. He had arranged for a maidservant to stand beside it and attend to her during her time at the banquet. Xerxes was a creator, always mindful of minute details; he wanted everything to be perfect. He pictured her walking through the entrance hall and stunning his guests with her beauty as she came to sit beside him. This beautiful scene captured his imagination as he anticipated her arrival.

The eunuchs' bowed heads and dragging steps communicated that something was amiss. Xerxes had assumed that this delay in the queen's appearance was the result of her insisting on changing her gown for him. Part of him loved this about her, and another part was irritated by it – no one should be allowed to keep him waiting for *this* long. He did not for even a moment consider that Vashti would openly defy him.

'Why this delay? Where is Queen Vashti?' demanded the king when the eunuchs remained silently bowed before him.

'I am afraid we have some disappointing news, Your Majesty,' said Mehuman, treading with caution. 'The queen has advised that she will not be able to attend the king's banquet at this time.'

'We did try to reason with the queen, Your Majesty,' Biztha added, in a bid to cover themselves, 'but she remained firm in her decision that it would be unbecoming of her as host and queen to leave her guests unattended.'

Xerxes quickly summoned the rest of the eunuchs and quizzed them on what had happened. They all gave him the same account. He could see they were trembling, clearly fearing the implications of their failure. He questioned whether they had in fact approached the queen, given that they viewed her as a goddess. He wondered if they had faltered in her presence and failed to make his request clear enough. However he quickly brushed this last thought aside as he knew that they were dependable and capable men. Part of him knew that Vashti could be strong-headed and insist on her own way. This trait he found attractive, and it would normally amuse him – but not today. His eyes roamed the room as he considered how he was going to announce that the queen would not be appearing. He knew that there was great anticipation about her arrival, and that they were looking forward to an opportunity to see her famed beauty up-close.

The king's demeanour turned from disbelief and shock to confusion and anger, which erupted in a silent fit of rage. His mouth suddenly felt dry, and he quickly beckoned for a drink. It was unheard-of for anyone to defy the king, and right now, in front of his guests, his *own wife* had done so. His head reeled, as he struggled to control his fury at this humiliation. *There will be consequences for your defiance, Vashti. I hope you are ready to face them!*

4

THE RULING

KING XERXES FELT AS if he had been struck by a physical blow in the core of his being, causing him to shudder. His nobles, seeing his obvious distress, quickly took over, and announced that Queen Vashti had been detained by commitments at the ladies' banquet and would unfortunately not be making an appearance. This was a very disappointing anti-climax for the guests. A few sensed that something serious was amiss, but most recovered from their disappointment and continued with the revelling.

The king took some deep breaths and recovered somewhat, pulling himself together. What was supposed to have been a highlight had turned into a massive humiliation, and he was not too sure how to handle it. He couldn't fathom what had made her publicly defy his request, and he was too disappointed and angry to think about facing her and hearing her explanation.

Xerxes suddenly felt drained. He wished it was all over, so that he could withdraw to somewhere quiet and be alone. His guests, on the other hand, seemed undeterred, determined to make the most of what was left of the banquet. The festivities continued unhampered, everyone in high spirits and not allowing the queen's non-appearance to spoil their merry-making. He was relieved to see this, in spite of his own extreme discomfort. As the clock ticked past midnight, the guests began to take their leave. Once the more respectable nobles had gone, and numbers had become acceptably low, the king bade the remainder farewell, and retreated to his office.

29

His study offered him the solitude he yearned for. He sank into a couch close to the fireplace, leaned back and spread out his long legs. He closed his eyes and, putting feelings of anger and humiliation aside, allowed his mind to slowly mull over the events of the past week. The banquet had undoubtedly been a success on many fronts. Not only had the celebration shown off the magnificence and bounty of his kingdom, but also it had cemented firm connections between himself and the nobles across the many provinces under his reign. He was pleased he had managed to interact with so many people from so many different walks of life during the tour. He felt a deep responsibility for leadership, and this had stirred him to renew his commitment to faithfully lead his subjects.

The king's mind now returned to Vashti's actions. While her behaviour had been inexcusable, he could not allow this single incident to detract from all the advantages he had won by hosting the banquet. But neither could he ignore her act of defiance. He was at a loss as how to handle the issue. He knew his nobles were probably discussing it amongst themselves at that very moment, and that his council would be deciding on befitting remedial action. Xerxes reflected on the possible consequences. Would this incident change the way his nobles viewed him? After all, his own wife had defied him right under their noses! He needed to assert his authority, but how? Vashti was not a threat to his life, nor was she an enemy of the kingdom; however, she had ignored his command. Sipping slowly on wine, he continued to search for an answer.

In the early hours of the morning, Xerxes left his study and made his way to his chambers, where he retired, tossing and turning in a restless sleep. He woke to the sound of birds singing, and became aware that he was still lying on top of the bed covers. He had not even removed his shoes. He quickly took stock, knowing without a doubt that this day was going to be pivotal in his reign. A decision regarding the queen's actions would have to be made.

His nobles would not take Vashti's refusal to heed his call lightly; she must be disciplined. Xerxes could not envision a satisfactory outcome; Vashti was, after all, the queen, and any remedial action would need to be fitting but not too demeaning.

Xerxes suspected that the council would request his presence at a meeting first thing. As he continued to lie there staring at the closed drapes, he decided to let things take their natural course. It was important for him to listen to their wise counsel, and to let these men resolve this issue. He knew in his spirit that change had to come; he only hoped that it would not cause too much upheaval in his kingdom's newly-established order.

Having made this decision, Xerxes rose from his bed and made his way to the bathroom, where he found his bath ready and waiting. He wasted no time in sinking into the hot water, welcoming the peace and quiet. The aromatic scent of his favourite bath-salts soothed his nerves. He dreaded the day ahead, so spent as much time as possible in the water. When he could postpone it no longer, he dried off and went into his dressing room, where his clothes were laid out. He noticed that his room had already been straightened out, and the drapes were now open. Looking out the window, he drank in the reassuring view of the mountains in the distance; it was a sight he looked forward to each morning. He could see his majestic white horse Pegasus grazing and occasionally swaying his tail from side to side. Nothing, he thought, could ever take away the joy of looking out over his kingdom.

Xerxes took his time, meticulously dressing in his royal robes. Once he had finished he took one last look at himself in the mirror. Making a stern face, he decided he looked like a king who was ready to face the day, despite the turmoil hidden in his spirit. He had to meet his council and hear their recommendations, and he knew that by this time they would be waiting for him in his main chambers.

Not far away, Queen Vashti was feeling relieved that the banquet was finally over, and she was pleased with the way it had turned out. Her guests had all given her glowing compliments, and she should have been feeling elated. She could not, however, shake off the uneasy feeling in the pit of her stomach. She was distracted, and continually paced the length of her room; this was something she would normally have done only when she was planning a party or trying to design an outfit for an event. This time, however, the reason for her pacing was different, and she hoped in her heart of hearts that the anxiety she felt was all for nothing, and that everything was going to be all right – or at least proceed with as little damage as possible.

The events of the previous evening played over and over in her mind, leaving a bad taste in her mouth. King Xerxes had required that she make an appearance at his banquet, and in the heat of the moment she had refused. The very thought of how she had defied the king now sent a shudder down her spine. She had done the unthinkable, and for what? Try as she might to justify her behaviour, she could not help but be appalled at her own defiance. She felt like kicking herself on the shins! She tried to calm herself down, but an increasing sense of uneasiness trickled into her spirit, forming a pool of fear which threatened to drown her.

Vashti's usually sparkling nature was now dimmed. She knew her husband's decisive nature, and could not be sure she would be safe, especially since his council and the eunuchs would be involved. If she could have reversed her actions, she would; but that was all water under the bridge now. She was going to have to face the music. But nothing could have prepared her for what lay ahead!

The council rose as Xerxes strode into the room. His freshly-groomed appearance gave no hint of the wreck he was inside. They respected him; he could not let them witness the turmoil this domestic issue was causing him. The musky fragrance of his cologne lingered as he passed them and took his seat. His steward brought him a cup of freshly-pressed grape juice, and he accepted it. He yearned for something stronger to settle his strained nerves, but he could not make such a request so early in the morning; grape juice would have to suffice.

Xerxes could tell the council was uneasy – their faces were as straight as their backs were rigid. He knew that whatever recommendation they had decided on would have been a difficult one for them. He realised that even though the final say lay with him, he was not going to be able to save Vashti from the mess she had created. He looked intently at these the wisest men in his kingdom, and prepared to listen with an open mind.

The king now invited them to give their recommendation on what should be done about the previous night's events. They did not mince their words. The queen had effectively defied the summons of the Crown itself, which amounted to nothing less than treason. Based on this reasoning, they built a case for her being considered a threat – not only to the king himself, but also to the entire kingdom. Queen Vashti had set a bad precedent, and the council would leave no stone unturned to ensure it never happened again. They believed that the only way to resolve the situation would be to dethrone her and banish her from the palace forever. This was their final, uncompromising recommendation.

On hearing this, the king's grief was great, and his heart felt a deep stab of pain. But he knew that these were men of wisdom, intelligence and great integrity, ones who truly had the interests of his kingdom at heart. He also realised that he could not let his love for his wife cloud his thinking. The council's recommendations had been harsh but reasonable, and he understood that what Vashti had done was wrong on all levels.

He felt dejected and defeated, powerless to save her from her fate. He still loved his wife, but he also knew that this one public act of defiance would be very difficult for him to recover from. Frustration and sadness were now fuming inside him – because he knew that there was no going back on it all. And so with a heavy heart the king accepted the council's recommendation – from that day on Vashti would no longer be queen, and was henceforth banished from the royal palace. All because of her disobedience to his call.

'Issue a decree throughout all the provinces,' King Xerxes ordered, 'proclaiming what will happen when anyone fails to obey the king!'

Vashti was inconsolable when she heard the news. There was to be no second chance. She had not even been given the opportunity to apologise! She appeared dazed as her mind tried to grasp the severity of her punishment. She was no longer queen; she was to be banished from the kingdom and replaced by another. The harsh verdict cut through her like a knife, as she saw her world shatter and collapse right before her own eyes. The life that she had grown accustomed to and loved, was being pulled out from under her like a rug. All the admiration and esteem was being ripped from her, and would be bestowed on another. She fell to her knees as if begging for a second chance, but there was nobody there to witness it. She had no one to plead with. She knew that begging the eunuchs for help would not get her anywhere, and she no longer had access to the king; it had always been the custom that the king could not be approached, not even by the queen herself, unless first summoned. She let out a deep, haunting, bitter wail of agony and regret. There was nothing more she could do.

'Pack your belongings,' was the stark order delivered by one of the eunuchs, 'and exit the royal chambers immediately.' This was the end then.

An agonising sense of shame engulfed Vashti, and a seizure of loud, heart-rending sobs racked her body. Crushed by despair, she doubted she could carry on under the weight of it. As queen, Vashti had become accustomed to servants waiting on her day and night, and was she was used to a life of absolute luxury. Did she now have it in her to survive the shame of being cast out? Suddenly coming to herself, she realised she had no option but to rouse herself, pack her things and leave. Vashti's eyes did not even have time to take in the beautiful furnishings that once had been hers, as she set about packing her belongings.

The usual sparkle and glow had drained out of Vashti as she exited the royal chambers. She appeared to have become gaunt and haggard overnight. This last ghostly image of her being escorted from the royal palace would haunt the many who witnessed her seemingly drift away. Not being able to face the crowd, she did not even turn for one last look at what had been her home for so long. Nor had she even had a chance to see King Xerxes one final time, to say goodbye. The last she had seen of him had been a few days before the banquets; he had been so busy planning his one, and she had been so focused on preparing for hers, that they had not had any time left over to spend together. And now it was too late!

Sitting in the dark musty carriage that had been allocated to take her away from the palace, with her head bowed, Vashti reflected on the nature of mistakes – errors of judgement – and their consequences. All that had been required of her that last evening was to make an appearance at the king's banquet. Thinking that her decision to disobey the king's request could be justified, understood and forgiven, she had grossly underestimated the outcome. At the time she could not have seen that it would be considered an unforgivable act of defiance and disobedience. This miscalculation had cost her *everything*.

As the world she had cherished faded into the distance, never to be seen again, Vashti faced a very different future. She was moving away from all that she had known and loved. She was going to have to find a way of re-establishing herself; it was not going to be easy.

5
—

THE STRATEGY

WITH THE PASSAGE OF time, King Xerxes' anger and pain subsided, and he eventually felt ready to face the daunting task of searching for a suitable queen to fill the void Vashti's exit had created. All he needed to do was signal his trusted confidants, and the wheels of action would no doubt be set in motion. The incident with Vashti had shaken him to the core, and his trust had taken a hard knock indeed. His mind trailed back to when he had met her; it had been love at first sight, and he still found it hard to believe that they had grown distant to the extent that she had not jumped at the opportunity of spending a short time with him at the banquet. He recalled how she used to find creative ways of being with him when protocol did not allow it. Xerxes could not imagine when her heart had started to grow less enchanted with him. Simply the thought of this made him sad.

Xerxes could not picture what he was looking for in a new queen, as Vashti had been his all. He knew that he needed someone who could understand her position in the kingdom – something which Vashti had failed to fully comprehend. So he decided to hold a meeting with his personal attendants, and to tap their wisdom. He did not want to reveal that he was at a loss as to how he was going to identify a new, more appropriate queen. His kingdom was vast, with a vibrant diversity of people. It was like finding a needle in a haystack!

But all the while the king was pondering, his trusted advisors had been one step ahead of him, and had already formulated a plan

36

of action. Xerxes was intrigued to find out that this elaborate plan to find a new queen was, in fact, already in its advanced stages. All that the council was waiting for was for him to get over his heartache, and for his seething anger to subside.

'We have selected and appointed a panel of commissioners from throughout the provinces to nominate candidates to be considered for the position of queen,' stated one of his advisors.

'Go on,' the king nodded.

'Suitable young ladies will be sent to the harem at the citadel of Susa.'

'Is that so?' interjected Xerxes.

'Yes, Your Majesty,' confirmed the advisor, with an emphatic nod. 'We thought the harem could be put to good use for this service. It is big enough to host the full complement of candidates, and having them all under one roof would be of great convenience. Hegai has already devised a schedule for grooming them for presentation. We have had the opportunity of going through it with him, and have every confidence that it will aid us in our quest to pick the rightful woman to sit beside you as your queen.'

'And what is this programme focusing on?' asked Xerxes with a blank expression on his face. It was quite difficult to tell if he was going to accept or reject their plans. The advisors were well prepared for this question, and one of them launched into the relevant details.

'Hegai's program will focus on refining both body and soul of the candidates. We know that it provides for an extensive beauty treatment schedule, one that will extend throughout their stay in the harem. In addition to this, they will also attend a personal development programme that will cover issues relating to etiquette, health and well-being, communication and social skills, and a variety of other topics appropriate for the nurturing of a future queen of the kingdom.'

'That sounds like a very comprehensive plan,' commented Xerxes.

'The programme has been structured to be both enjoyable and interactive. The candidates will be under close scrutiny; our intention is to present to you only those we feel have potential,' continued the advisor, well satisfied with the king's reaction.

'It is quite evident that you have put a great deal of thought into this,' said Xerxes. 'You may proceed with the programme; you have my full support.'

The advisors were both pleased and relieved that the king had approved of their plan. This being done, the king now relaxed, never imagining that this simple exercise would end up causing such a stir!

6
—

THE SEARCH

HEGAI HAD ARRANGED FOR groups of women to be checked into the harem each month. This was to ensure that each of the provinces had equal opportunity to put forward suitable candidates. This cycle would continue until the entire kingdom had been covered, and the future queen identified.

For the entire duration of their stay the women would receive extensive beauty treatments. During the first six months they would be bathed in oil of myrrh and other special salts, followed by a second six months of treatments with various perfumes and cosmetics. They would be soaked, bathed, steamed and scrubbed to ensure that they were looking their best when their turn came to be presented to the king.

From the outset the search was for more than outer beauty alone; Vashti was evidence that it would take more than just this to make a good queen. Hegai was on the lookout for those who displayed maturity, and who had emotional stability and mental strength. Various pressure tests were used to determine these qualities, and to determine who stayed and who left.

The women were coached on matters of etiquette – how to sit, walk, speak and dress. A typical day could start with early-morning devotions, followed by a period of meditation. They would then go outside for some exercise in the harem grounds. After this they would retire to the beauty spa, where they would go through the procedure of the day. The girls were all placed on a special diet that had been carefully planned for them, in order to ensure that they were healthy and vibrant. Each day Hegai required that they read extensively on a wide variety of topics; this ensured that they were kept abreast of current issues, and also allowed for them to indulge their individual passions. No two days were alike, and the time simply flew by.

The days in the harem were packed with different activities and, unbeknownst to the women, Hegai was singling out those who showed potential. He hovered over his charges with an eagle eye, ensuring that only the best ones progressed to the next stage. The king got the opportunity to meet the women only once they had gone through all the beauty treatments and Hegai was satisfied with their general progress.

He deliberately put them through tasks to assess how they handled different situations; some found them fun and games, whilst others were stretched beyond their comfort zone. Hegai was gentle but firm in the way he handled them, ensuring each one was given the chance to prove her worth. Most of them left of their own accord, either after suffering frustration or from buckling under the pressure to do well. However, others Hegai had to let go of as gently as he could – when it became clear that this journey was not for them.

Hegai had the girls instructed on the various cultures of the kingdom, and then engaged with them in order to test how much knowledge they had acquired. It quickly became apparent just who were interested in issues affecting the kingdom and who were not. Prior to being selected for the programme, many of the women had mistakenly thought it would be their appearance that would land them the prized crown; however, most of these failed to make it past the character test, despite the apparent effects of the beauty treatments. Hegai needed to make sure that those who remained were emotionally stable and had strong potential for leadership. After all, the one chosen would be the next queen!

$$\underline{7}$$

ESTHER

ESTHER ENTERED THE HAREM with the last intake for the year.
She appeared to be an ordinary girl, and it was clear that she
came from a humble background. The sandals on her feet were
practical rather than frivolous, and her garments were made of
durable fabric. Most of the other girls came from wealthier fami-
lies, judging by their more fashionable garments and the amount
of luggage they brought in with them. Four girls were to share a
room; they all had separate beds and cupboards, but there was a
communal bathroom. Everything that Esther had brought for her
stay was packed into one small case. She quickly unpacked the little she had, neatly folding it into the cupboard space allocated to
her. She had plenty of space to spare, whereas some of the women
could not even fit in half of their belongings. But she did not seem
deterred by her comparative lack of possessions, and always had a
ready smile on her face, and treated everyone with grace.

Esther was of slender build, and had long hair that was neatly
pulled away from her face and tied in a bun. She had a flawless
skin, and her engaging smile revealed dimples on both sides of her
face, one just a little deeper than the other. Her soft, musical voice
made her come across as gentle and friendly. Hegai, in the few
direct interactions he had had with her, noticed that she bought a
warm glow into every space she entered. He had a feeling that she
was a caring person, and made a note to keep his eye on her. She

had an air of simple sophistication, and his mind went back to his first encounter with her.

'Hello Esther, welcome to the harem,' he had greeted her on the day of her arrival.

'Thank you, Sir; it is an honour to be here,' she had responded softly. 'This is a very beautiful place,' she added, clear admiration showing on her face. 'I look forward to my time here.'

'What do you think of your room?' he had enquired.

'It looks beautiful and most comfortable,' she had replied. 'I look forward to meeting my room-mates '

'They should be here shortly,' he had responded. 'They are still travelling from their provinces.' And, seeing that she was a little uneasy in her new surroundings, he then added, 'Let me show you around the rest of the place. After all, this is going to be your home for the next few months.'

They then had gone on a quick tour of the grounds, which in turn had prompted Esther to ask a lot of questions about all the activities that were planned. Hegai had explained as they went, eventually releasing her to go and rest in her room and recover from her long journey.

Esther quickly fell into the regular routine of the programme, and was eager to learn everything that came her way. She had a passion for reading, and was always found deep in study whenever there was a break from group activities. A whole new world was opening to her, and she was fascinated by all she was discovering.

Hegai was well pleased with her progress. He had purposely devised the girls' daily schedules to be packed with varying activities, so that he could see just how well they adapted to different scenarios, and also measure their reaction to pressure. It was quite easy to distinguish the ones who were coping from the ones who were not.

Esther proved to be a pillar of strength to her peers. As she settled into her new life, it was clear to see that she took a keen interest in those around her. In a short time she knew the names of all the other women, and she went out of her way to assist them whenever they were struggling; a natural-born encourager, she wanted everyone to do well. She had an inner strength and beauty that was starting to become apparent to all those who encountered her. She also proved to be an exceptionally good listener, and seemed to have a knack for asking the right questions. Always ready with a word of encouragement, her speech was laced with profound wisdom and understanding, at a level unusual for one her age. Everyone warmed to her, and found her a true delight to be around. As she continued gaining the trust and respect of her peers, many of the girls approached her for help with one thing or another.

Hegai took note of all of this in silence. He was intrigued that she seemed unaware of the strength and beauty she carried. She had an innocence that seemed to be lacking in many of the others.

Esther lay awake, pondering on her stay in the harem. The events of the past few months played randomly on her mind, and she smiled to herself as she realised how far she had come. She enjoyed the early-morning devotions, as well as the exercise routines and the beauty treatments. Then the lectures and study, as well as the demonstrations of practical skills such as cooking, gardening and sewing all added variety to the day. She smiled in amusement as she imagined what her mother would have made of all this; she had spent more time in the past few months focusing on improving herself than she had done in her entire lifetime!

Esther reflected on the new world that was slowly opening up to her, and how completely different it was to the one she had been accustomed to. Her day-to-day life had revolved around keeping the home clean, putting food on the table, and looking after anyone who needed it. She was lucky to have had parents who had been hard-working and full of faith, and who had been strong pillars, not only for her but also her extended family and the community at large. Her father had been a carpenter by trade, and the house they had lived in before going into exile had been built by him, as had all the furniture in it. Every night they sat at a table he had made and ate food her mother had grown. Her mother had been a renowned seamstress, and she also had tended their livestock and fields, the latter being sown with a variety of crops that had not only fed them but also provided produce for sale at the village market. Thus they had never lacked anything; but neither could they have been considered rich.

Esther's approach to life was a blend of her parents' – she was hard-working and selfless. She had always taken a keen interest in the projects her father had undertaken, assisting him in his work wherever she could. Together there had never been an idle moment in their lives. She had always admired the love her parents had had for each other, and how they had shared the little they had had with family and friends. Anyone who had visited their homestead would have been sure to leave with something freshly picked from the garden or field. Her parents had been generous givers, and had not held back whenever anyone had been in need.

Her parents' untimely deaths had left the entire community shaken and Esther an orphan. Her much-loved uncle Mordecai had not hesitated to step up and take her in as his own. As she had gradually recovered from the tragedy, she had continued living her life with an attitude of gratitude that she still had someone who loved and cared for her. Mordecai had continued what her parents had started, and had raised her to be a young lady of faith. He had also taught her to praise and worship in all circumstances. He had spoken to her about their journey from Israel into captivity in the land of Persia, where she now was a foreigner in a land with strange customs. He had taught her that they should not conform to the things that compromised their religion; instead they should hold on to their faith. At times this had been difficult, but Mordecai had assured her that they were under Divine protection, and that there would always be a way through, even when it seemed that there was none. He had praised and worshipped his way through this difficult transition, and she had joined him in this.

His words now echoed in her mind: *Esther, we are heading into captivity, but we are under command to flourish in that environment. We are not to stop dreaming and believing for the best. We are to reach out for new opportunities, as everything that we put our minds to will prosper.* She recalled how his face had lit up with conviction as he had spoken these words to her. Her uncle was a man of great faith, and she loved him dearly.

The days in the harem seemed to fly by, and the appointed time for Esther to be ushered into the presence of the king approached fast. She was surprised at herself; whereas she had once felt over-awed at the thought of meeting him, she now felt confident and well prepared. She considered the king to be a tower of strength in the kingdom, and felt honoured to have earned the opportunity to be considered worthy of being near him. She did not ever think he would pick her as his queen – there were so many amazing women lined up for him. But because she thought that this would be the only chance she would ever get to sit and chat with him, she decided she would use the time to ask about all the things she had long been curious about – his kingdom, his reign and himself!

Esther was by now proficient at dressing herself up, putting on her make-up and doing her hair, and she no longer felt the need to have a train of maids waiting on her as the other girls did. However, she accepted Hegai's advice for the upcoming preparations, and agreed on keeping the assistance of one maid and putting on a simple gown and minimal make-up. He had also suggested that she wear her favourite pieces of jewellery – a single strand of pearls with matching earrings – and that her hair be arranged high on her head, with a few curls escaping on the sides. He wanted to show off Esther's natural beauty, and discouraged her from making any embellishments. She did not mind these directions at all, as she respected his knowledge and judgement.

Esther left the harem late in the afternoon. She was taken to the palace and ushered into the chambers that had been prepared for her. Her maid had a room close to hers, and she drew some comfort from this. At that moment her maid was the only person she knew in the palace, and she wanted her to stay with her for as long as possible. Esther was amazed by the sheer size of her chambers, and she appreciated the freshly-cut flowers that had been placed in a huge vase on a table near the entrance to her dressing room. Most of the furniture in the room was made of oak, including the large four-poster bed that sat in the middle of the room. She instinctively ran her fingers over the plush purple bed-cover, feeling its soft, luxurious material under her touch. The bedroom had large windows which were adorned with heavy drapes that were currently drawn back. Esther moved to the window, and gazed out on a stunning view of the gardens. The scent of roses drifted her way, and her eyes feasted on the rich fusion of colour. She dreamed that she would someday have an opportunity to wander through all this splendour.

She was brought back to earth by the thought that this would probably be the only time she was ever going to see these gardens. After all, what chance did she stand of ever coming back to the palace? She stood there breathing in the perfume for a few moments longer, as if to take in as much as she could with this one opportunity that she had been given.

Esther's train of thought was interrupted by her maid announcing that her bath was ready; it was now time for her to start getting ready for her royal 'date'. Just the thought of it sent a shiver of excitement down her spine. Considering where she had come from, she could never have imagined that she would one day find herself preparing to dine with the king!

As she bathed, Esther's mind went back to her parents, and then to Mordecai, who had taken her in as his own and had taught her so many things, taking over from where her parents had left off. She trusted him and looked up to him, even when she did not quite understand his reasoning. He had told her never to reveal her ethnicity to anyone, and she had obeyed without questioning; she knew that her uncle was gifted with foresight, and she had respected his wishes. The only thing she found baffling, and if not a little amusing, was that he had put her forward for this selection process because he believed that she had every chance of becoming the future queen!

Dressing up was not too much of an effort for Esther. Her maid helped her to secure the straps at the back of the elegant, purple, satin gown that had been created specifically for her. It was short-sleeved, with a v-shaped, wrap-over bodice which tapered down to a close-fitting waistline, all held in place with a beaded belt. Her lightly-gathered satin skirt swept to the floor, making her look tall and elegant. It shimmered when she moved, highlighting the simple strand of pearls around her neck. The only accessory that she would carry with her to dinner was a sparkling, purple clasp bag with gold-coloured latches. When she was ready to make her way to the king, she gave her maid a parting wave and simply said, 'Pray for me.'

As Esther began to move through her chambers, her mind filled with the possibilities of what the evening might hold. Her face was a little flushed, as she tried to imagine her first encounter with the king. She wanted to make a good first impression, and hoped that she would be able to hold it together throughout their meeting. She was half afraid that she might panic and clam up, or even perhaps start babbling! She tried to recall some of the words of encouragement that Mordecai had given her, but her mind simply went blank. As she entered her lounge, she saw that the escort was already waiting to accompany her on her short journey through the palace to the king. She greeted him with her usual smile, which he acknowledged, and they departed. He walked ahead of her all the way, and she followed, lost in her own thoughts and aware that there was no turning back now!

The journey to the king's lounge was quite different to Esther's walk to her chambers. Back then she had had time to notice and enjoy all the intricate details; now the outside world was a blur, and she retreated within herself, her mind barely registering and her pulse racing. She held tightly onto her clutch bag, her cool, silky gloves a balm to her sweating palms.

The escort ushered Esther into a grand lounge. Captivated by the beauty and magnificence around her, she quickly forgot her panic. She could not believe that the interior of a building could be so elegantly and intricately adorned. She was simply spellbound. Deep admiration of it all, from the beautifully-decorated walls to the high painted ceilings and the opulent furniture, reflected on her face. Like all the other rooms of the palace, the lounge had huge windows which bathed the grand room in natural light and afforded breathtaking views of the gardens which surrounded them. Esther acknowledged in her heart the generations who had contributed to this beauty – it was beyond anything she could have imagined.

<u>8</u>

First Impressions

King Xerxes sat behind the desk in his study; he had resolved to leave his work for now, and to wait where he was until the upcoming meeting.

Some time back he had carried out an extensive renovation of this wing of the palace, cleverly including a study for himself just above the lounge and dining area. This worked well for him, as he could on occasion be called upon to attend to urgent matters whilst entertaining guests in the main lounge. In the past he would have had to excuse himself and go to his office at the other end of the palace, whereas now the study served this purpose. It was furnished with a stately-looking desk, and a matching cabinet filled with neat rows of parchments and scrolls. There were couches and an immaculate rug set before a huge fireplace. A cabinet filled with the king's favourite drinks was placed at one end, and over it hung a huge portrait of himself. On the other walls there were similarly-large portraits of both of his parents and other deceased family members. Vashti herself had been represented on this wall, but her portrait had been hastily taken down soon after her dismissal. It was not hard to see where her picture had hung – now all that was left was was an empty space with a huge peg stuck in the wall.

Xerxes felt a familiar tug of tension as he recalled issuing instructions for Vashti's portrait to be removed and given to her before she exited the palace. He pushed these memories of her to the back of his mind, poured a drink, and gazed with unseeing

49

eyes at the lounge below. Tonight he was scheduled to dine with a woman named Esther. This was all he knew about her and he had been given no other details. He could not imagine what she might be like, and he hoped that the evening would not be filled with awkward silences in which he would be expected to think on his feet and keep the conversation going. This had often happened on previous occasions, as many of the women had become tongue-tied in his presence, and had ended up simply staring at him in intimidation. He was quite frankly starting to lose patience with it all, and had every intention of calling a meeting with Hegai to see what could be done. A small part of him suspected that he may have set his expectations of the future queen a little too high; he wondered if anyone could realistically meet them.

The wall between the study and overlooking the lounge was one big expanse of glass, covered by blinds that were partially opened. This way he had a full view of the interior of the lounge, whereas anyone there could not see back into the study. Xerxes had designed it this way as he often required privacy to attend to matters of state. Looking into the main lounge at this moment, his interest was not particularly piqued by the sight of Esther being escorted in. He could tell her hair was jet black, and that she carried herself with elegance. Clearly Hegai's grooming programme was working well.

9

The Meeting

Esther was amazed at the layout of the room that she had just been ushered into. She had never seen anything so regal and elegant in her entire life. There was so much beauty in this space that she felt goosebumps form on her bare arms. The wooden floors had been polished to a deep shine, and there was the faint scent of lavender, which she presumed came from the floor polish. Strategically placed around the room were several huge vases filled with the biggest arrangements of flowers she had ever set eyes on. Everything looked so spotless and precise that she felt as if she was standing on an elaborate stage. Her knees suddenly started shaking and, feeling overwhelmed and afraid she might faint and knock over something valuable, she looked for the nearest place to sit. Having found a suitable chair, she closed her eyes and drew in deep breaths in an attempt to calm herself down.

Esther remained seated and allowed her eyes to once again roam over everything that surrounded her. Her current setting was a stark contrast to the modest home she had grown up in. She imagined her parents' entire two-bedroom house could have easily fitted into this huge lounge. Their home had been furnished with offcuts from her father's projects. Every piece of furniture had had its own story, and she had never grown tired of listening to him telling and re-telling them to anyone who would listen. Esther had seen this furniture slowly take on the form and shape of his design drawings, and each item was simple and exquisite. But she could never have imagined that she would one day be surrounded by this amount of opulence and beauty. She suddenly wished that her father could be there to see what she was seeing. She knew he would have enjoyed telling her in minute detail just how each item had been made. She guessed, a nostalgic smile coming over her face, that he would also have known the value of each of them. An involuntary sigh escaped from her lips as she realised how much she missed her parents.

By now Esther had calmed down considerably, and something that looked like a glass tank filled with water caught her eye. Without a second thought, she stood up and walked the length of the room to get a closer look. She was amazed to discover that it was indeed just that, and that it had fish swimming in it! It was the first time she had seen fish swimming anywhere other than in a pond or lake. At the bottom of the tank there were pieces of driftwood and gravel, and above this, green plants gently swayed in the water, making it an ideal natural habitat for the fish that swam lazily around in the beautiful enclosure. She was fascinated as she watched them swim back and forth in front of her. She kept her eyes on one particularly colourful one that was quite different from all the others in the tank. Its beautiful fusion of blue, green and purple stripes was easy to follow, and the rest of them looked plain in comparison. She wondered what else lay in store for her. *I'll have to tell Mordecai about this*, she thought. She could not wait to inform him of all the beautiful things she had seen in this magnificent palace.

Esther continued watching the fish for a while longer, before moving to have a closer look at a huge portrait of a regal-looking woman who had gentle eyes and the hint of a smile on her lips. She was wearing a royal gown that was complemented by an intricate diamond-encrusted necklace. The artist had captured a sparkle on the central diamond, emphasising the riches this lady wore with such apparent ease. In that split second, Esther felt like an imposter. The gnawing feeling gave rise to a sudden feeling of inadequacy.

Maybe I was chosen by mistake, my name picked by accident. I clearly have a foreign background and upbringing; what am I doing here? These thoughts, and others besides, taunted her as she stood in these luxurious surroundings.

A feeling of uneasiness churned in the pit of her stomach, causing a wave of panic to start rising within her, and she doubted she could ever hope to measure up to the king's expectations. Her mouth was now dry, and her breathing rapid and shallow. Her eyes were suddenly drawn to a lace curtain that fluttered in the slight breeze entering through the open windows, and she immediately crossed the floor to inhale deeply of the fresh evening air.

Recovering somewhat, she looked out on bush upon bush of colourful roses that filled the garden. This wondrous sight had a calming effect on her, and the feeling of panic slowly subsided. Gazing past the gardens, she caught sight of a magnificent white horse grazing in the next field. She had never set eyes on a creature so elegant and beautiful, and she longed to run her fingers through its silky mane.

Xerxes had been watching Esther as she explored her surroundings, and was still studying her now as she stood gazing out of the window. She looked like a picture, the sun's evening rays catching her dark hair. He could see a smile forming on her lips, and he wondered what she was looking at with so much concentration. He tried to follow her gaze, but his view was blocked; he imagined she was simply admiring the gardens.

A sudden knock on the door confirmed that it was time to go down and meet his guest for the evening. This had by now become routine for the king, and he went down the stairs in a brisk and business-like manner. His thoughts strayed back to his preparations for the next day's events. There were still a few points he needed to incorporate into the speech he was working on. Tonight's dinner would not take too long; he would return and continue his preparation as soon as it was over.

Esther was still gazing at the horse as King Xerxes entered the lounge. She turned her face towards the sound of the approaching footsteps, and saw him coming towards her. Her heart started hammering in her chest, and she stood rooted to the spot, unable to move. To make matters worse, everything that Hegai had taught her about respectfully receiving the king had suddenly disappeared. She desperately tried to hold things together.

'Welcome, Esther,' the king greeted her, towering over her as he joined her at the window.

'Your Majesty,' she said, remembering her manners and curtsying deeply, her head tilted a little on one side.

'I hope my staff have been taking good care of you?' he enquired, as she raised herself up again.

'Yes, thank you, Your Majesty. They have been very attentive,' Esther responded.

She was trying hard not to stare at him directly, but at the same time wanted to have a good look. She was still very nervous, and her hand shook slightly as she extended it towards the king. Hegai had drilled her repeatedly on how to greet the king, but in her mild panic she had automatically reverted to her own custom of greeting – the extension of one hand, not two. Colour flooded her face as she realised what she had just done. King Xerxes had not commented, but she had noticed the slight look of surprise on his face, and she chided herself. *You must focus, Esther! He is the king, after all.*

Xerxes stood beside Esther, joining her in observing the scenery outside. His heart swelled with pride as he noticed Pegasus grazing in the field, and he realised that she had been admiring his pride and joy.

'He is really beautiful,' Esther commented.

'He is one of a kind,' agreed the king, turning to nod at the servant standing nearby, as an indication that they were ready to dine.

The palace chefs were under strict instruction to create a unique dining experience for the king and his guests, and the now elaborately-laid table was testament to this. They stood around stiffly, waiting for his nod of satisfaction with their handiwork. It was always interesting for them when he had new company. They sometimes caught rare glimpses of him being relaxed and friendly, but more often he remained distant and mechanical. Noticing the rigid way he now stood, and the impatient tapping of his foot, they suspected that it was not going to go well for this latest guest. Dinner was always over in a short space of time whenever the king was in this type of a mood.

Moving towards the table with Esther in tow, Xerxes again thought of the more important matters that awaited him after dinner. Months of trying to find the next queen had taken its toll on him, and his patience was wearing thin to the point of breaking.

10

ESTHER AND XERXES

XERXES PULLED OUT THE chair for Esther, and courteously waited as she eased herself into it. She had a slight flush on her face at the thought of the king helping her into her seat. He appeared not to have noticed this as he strode purposefully to his side of the table. Casting a brief glance across the table at his companion, he realised with some exasperation that he had not received adequate background information on her. He didn't know anything about her, other than her name.

The head chef entered and announced the first item on the menu – creamy mushroom soup. This was served up in elaborately-practised fashion by two servants, who then promptly disappeared into the adjoining room, leaving their diners in peace. Xerxes hoped the food would be up to the usual high standard, as he did not want to be embarrassed in any way. He was not particularly concerned about Esther, but he wanted to keep up the good reputation of palace hospitality, as the candidates came from far and wide.

Esther thanked the waiters with a warm smile, and then turned to the head chef. 'This soup looks scrumptious,' she said. 'Where did you pick the mushrooms?'

The mushrooms were freshly picked this afternoon, from high up in the hills close to the palace,' he informed her, bowing slightly. He was flattered that the king's guest had taken an interest in the dish he had prepared. A slight smile of amusement had begun to form on Xerxes' lips, and he wondered what other surprises the evening would hold.

The day had been long, and Esther felt hungry. Following Xerxes' lead, she delicately picked up her spoon and tasted the contents of her bowl. It was delicious and, finding comfort in the food brought out courage in her soul, she did not hold back on her compliments.

'This is delicious,' she said. 'I have never had soup this good. It must have taken hours to prepare.'

'Wait until you try the sauce on the steak,' the king assured her.

'I am sure it will be sublime,' was Esther's relaxed response. 'But I can't help wondering how far they must have travelled to find these mushrooms,' she added as an afterthought.

Xerxes found Esther's line of thinking both amusing and somewhat refreshing at the same time; he realised that he rarely gave a second thought to these simple things that she was commenting on. They continued to enjoy their soup in silence.

'The palace is bigger and far more beautiful than I could ever have imagined,' Esther commented, almost to herself. 'Those gardens out there are so beautiful; I think I could easily lose track of time exploring and relaxing in them.' She stopped, and almost kicked herself under the table, as she suddenly realised she was expressing random thoughts in the presence of the king!

Fortunately Xerxes now joined in with her easily – keeping the palace gardens well cared for was dear to his heart, and he knew them like the back of his hand. He responded to her questions about the vegetable garden with interest. He shared details about the different sections it comprised, the varieties of vegetables they grew, what was currently in season, and what he planned for the next harvest. He had an elaborate knowledge of the sowing and reaping schedules of the many different crops. In fact he had an amazing ability for working with his hands, whether it be harvesting the produce or decorating the palace. Esther was pleasantly surprised when she realised that King Xerxes and her late father had something in common: an ability to create things of beauty. She could not have imagined that the king would have found the time for mundane activities such as gardening. After all, he had so many servants to do these things for him; surely he had more important matters to deal with?

'Gardening has always been my passion,' he said, 'even as a young boy.' He seemed to have read her thoughts. 'The simplicity of the garden, and the joy of watching things grow, provides an opportunity for me to step away from complex issues and to recharge.'

Esther wondered if the king had any questions for her – she had so many more for him; the garden was only the beginning! She now felt relaxed, and had completely forgotten how rattled and anxious she had been not so long before. She was amazed at the side of King Xerxes that was slowly opening up to her.

'What do you think of the flower garden?' the king asked, picking up on her earlier comment. She responded by giving him an account of the various flowers and bushes that she had seen in the palace gardens, and which ones she liked the best. The conversation slowly moved from the garden to the grand lounge itself, and finally to the fish tank with its colourful fish that had fascinated her. There was no mistaking that she had an eye for beauty. And he sensed that she was calm and enjoying herself in his presence.

King Xerxes recalled how some of the other candidates had stammered or had spilled their soup – all because they had been focusing too hard on their performance, rather than on enjoying their surroundings. His earlier exasperation with the process had started to melt away, and he felt relaxed and himself in Esther's company. He did not notice that the meal was taking some time to get through; as far as he was concerned, they had all the time in the world to chat and enjoy the excellent food.

Xerxes did not ask many personal questions about Esther's background or upbringing, as this was information he should have been furnished with before meeting her. He imagined Esther assumed he must know all about her from Hegai, and asking her now about things he should already know would be inappropriate and awkward. In the case of all the other candidates, he had been apprised of their personal details prior to meeting with them. For some unknown reason, this had not happened with Esther.

As the evening wore on, the stoic and regal image that Esther had built up of the king began to crumble. In its place was a real man, one who had immense power but who at the same time was gentle, humorous and genuine. She realised that she was enjoying his company immensely. At first she had been tense, worried that she would make a spectacle of herself; now she was surprised at how relaxed and at ease she felt. Even her close proximity to him did not intimidate her as much as she imagined it would. The evening was going very well so far, much to her relief and surprise.

Esther now looked directly at the king as they talked, and she noticed his formal attire, his well-trimmed hair, and his close-shaven beard. He exuded strength and power, and she wondered about him. As the meal progressed she asked him questions about the kingdom – albeit hesitantly, as she was uncertain if he would be willing to share such important matters with her. Much to her amazement, he answered her openly and honestly.

For his part, the king was surprised at the interest Esther showed in matters of state. He was impressed by her knowledge about many different social issues, and her questions and comments showed that she was a critical thinker and that she had a passion for issues of justice and peace. He also could not help but note how courteous and respectful she was with the servants – she complimented them and gave them warm smiles as they bustled around. Although he was not aware of it at that moment, his wounded and cynical heart was beginning to thaw. He was enjoying Esther's company immensely.

The time seemed to speed by and, although he did not want to admit it, he felt a little disappointed that their evening together was coming to an end. As it was getting late, he suggested that they leave in order to allow the servants space to clear up.

'How about a drink?' he suggested, gently guiding Esther to a more comfortable seat in the spacious lounge. He was not feeling hurried anymore, and was grateful for her company. Turning to his servant, he said, 'I'll have my usual cup of strong, black tea.' He then looked at Esther. 'And you?'

'A cup of hot ginger and honey, please,' she replied softly. 'It's my favourite.'

Their conversation continued long after their drinks were finished. Esther was thoroughly enjoying listening to the king and having her curiosity about many matters quenched. She discovered that he had a delightful sense of humour. He recounted stories and escapades which she could not imagine him telling just anyone; he seemed to have lowered his guard with her, and she guessed she was witnessing a side of him not seen by many.

As midnight approached, Xerxes had to force himself to let her go. He could see signs of tiredness about her face, despite her continued animation. Apart from this, he had an early-morning meeting coming up in a few hours, followed by an important inspection that needed to be undertaken. He informed her that he wanted to have dinner with her again the following evening, something he had not done with any of the other contestants. Esther had not anticipated this development, and was a little uncertain as to how she should respond; so she neither accepted nor declined the invitation, instead indicating that all arrangements would be made through Hegai. Satisfied with this, King Xerxes bade her goodnight, and one of the palace ushers escorted her to her quarters.

There was much speculation amongst the servants over Esther's visit with the king. They believed that his interest had been piqued, but they could not be certain of the outcome. Judging by the length of the dinner, together with the lounge conversation that had been spiced with peals of laughter, they were hopeful that they might see her again. They had all enjoyed serving her, and had appreciated the way in which she had spoken to them, complimenting them and giving them warm, cheerful smiles. They had seen something in her that they had not seen in any of the other ambitious candidates who had come through the doors since the search for a new queen had begun. Moreover, they were all delighted to see their king relaxed and laughing once again.

11

A Flicker of Something New

As Esther lay in bed that night, she wondered about the king. Before meeting him, she had imagined he would be lofty and unapproachable, not easily spoken to. She was surprised at how the evening had flown by. Images of him kept playing in her head. She had been sitting close to him all evening, and she had wished the night could have gone on and on; she could not remember when she had last enjoyed the company of anyone so much. She now found herself looking forward to seeing him again the following night. Although she knew he had enjoyed her company too, she could not see herself as a serious contender for the position of queen, still believing that there were worthier candidates to fill such a high calling. The thought that he would likely pick someone else did nothing at all to dampen her spirits.

Reflecting further on the king, Esther called to mind her father's loving description of his own father, her grandfather. He had described him as being as bold as a lion, as strong as an ox, as majestic as an eagle, and as gentle as a dove; all four distinct qualities blended into one personality. She now recognised these same strengths in the king. She had known from all the great stories she had heard about him that he had a reputation for being bold and strong, but tonight she had had the opportunity to see his other, finer qualities – he had piercing insight, and had shown a gentle, even playful, side to his nature.

Esther let out a small sigh of contentment. She felt happy that she had had the opportunity to spend the evening with such a great man, and looked forward to spending more time with him. Talking to him was like exploring a treasure chest, and she very much wanted to discover more! Just being in his presence made her realise that there was much good in the kingdom, and she felt sure she could play some part in helping bring further peace and prosperity to it. There was so much work to be done, and the king could not be expected to do it all by himself. He had ignited in her a passion to serve the kingdom, whether she was chosen as queen or not, and she resolved to start playing her small part. As she drifted off to sleep, her mind was still on the king, and she knew her life would never quite be the same again.

At the other end of the palace, Xerxes was still wide awake. After leaving her he had headed back up the stairs into his study. Normally he would have gone straight to his sleeping chambers, but tonight he needed to figure things out. The woman he had met tonight was different to all the others. She had managed to make him feel relaxed and free to open up about his world. He loved how she had hung on his every word, and how she had asked surprisingly thoughtful questions. His heart told him that there was depth in her, and his mind searched for a reason for this. He feared that Hegai may have advised her on the right questions to ask; but surely she could not have rehearsed everything. Xerxes dismissed the thought as impossible, as he remembered how passionate she had been about the welfare of his people. He felt challenged by some of the questions she had raised when they had chatted about things that would not have been of interest to any ordinary person, certainly not to most of the women he had dined with recently. He remembered the passion that he had seen in her eyes as she had raised certain issues with him.

The king returned to his work and tried to concentrate on his speech preparation, but Esther's image floated before his eyes. He smiled, enjoying seeing her in his imagination, her dark hair held up by a silvery clasp, loose strands framing her face and accentuating her beautiful brown eyes. He loved her delicate nose, her pearly white teeth and her long neck. He remembered admiring her flowing gown as he had steered her from the dining table to the couch. He loved everything about her, and he was amused that the word 'like' was slowly being replaced with 'love' in his mind. He remembered how delicately she had held her cup as she sipped her tea, and how slender her hands were – and he suddenly wondered if he had been staring at her. He wondered too what impression he had made on her; had she found him overbearing, or possibly too old? This last thought made him break out into a cold sweat; a part of him *wanted* her to like him, and he was so looking forward to seeing her again the following evening.

Xerxes again tried turning his attention back to his speech, but he could not concentrate on the words in front of him. He simply couldn't get Esther out of his mind – her fragrance, her soft voice, her probing questions, her abandoned laughter at his jokes, her whispers of disbelief at some of the issues that he had to deal with as king, and her sighs of concern and sadness at some of the more emotional issues that he had experienced. He put the parchment away, got up from his couch, and slowly went back down the stairs, his mind and senses still taken up with her. He realised that he would need to tread very carefully and see how this second meeting turned out – he could not allow himself to wonder if she was the one for him after a single very pleasant evening!

Hegai felt hopeful when he received word that the king had requested Esther's company at dinner the following evening. He made the necessary arrangements to ensure that she was dressed in a manner befitting the occasion, arranging for another gown and matching ensemble to be packed and despatched to her room, with instructions for her to attend a second dinner with the king. Esther was astounded when she laid eyes on the gown chosen for her to wear; it looked too magnificent for her. The aide who delivered it gave her chambermaid strict instructions to make sure she was dressed and prepared immaculately for her second meeting with the king. The day passed quickly, and by the time she was ready to set out for the evening she looked like nothing less than an angel in her attire; she even seemed to float over the ground as she walked.

Xerxes drew in a sharp breath when he laid eyes on her. She looked dazzling, and appeared to have a warm, shimmering glow surrounding her. She was wearing an elegant dusky-pink dinner dress, with a contrasting lace yoke and long sleeves; its soft colour bought out the glowing beauty of her skin. Her hair was loosely tied on the top of her head, revealing a pair of pearl earrings that matched her necklace. She wore only the faintest hint of make-up, which made Xerxes feel that he wanted to keep on discovering the true nature of her face. She looked like a perfect rose, and had a sweet, fragrant perfume to match. He was enchanted by her appearance and intoxicated by her scent.

The conversation during the evening flowed naturally, and they simply picked up from where they had left off the previous night. The time flew by as they talked on a range of different topics. It felt as if they had known each other all their lives. As he did before, Xerxes again invited her to his lounge, where they could relax and share a drink.

Esther sipped slowly from her cup, and enjoyed the king's company. She was, by now, quite comfortable in his presence, and pleased to have the opportunity to have another good look at him. She liked the way he was dressed; whereas he had seemed a little formal and business-like the previous night, this evening he appeared more relaxed. He again was wearing dark robes made of expensive cloth, but she noticed there was less adornment this time, making him appear more casual. She could even catch a faint hint of the masculine musk perfume that he had applied, and she found herself looking forward to it drifting her way more often. She loved the laughter lines that formed around his eyes when he laughed or smiled and, above all, she loved the way he fully engaged with her during their conversations. She had no way of stopping the attraction that was slowly building up inside her.

Xerxes had intentionally cleared his schedule for the following morning, as he had suspected that he was going to have a late night with Esther. When the temperature in the lounge grew cooler, he lit the fire that had been prepared for them. He would normally have left this for a servant to do, but this evening he had dismissed everyone early as he wanted her all to himself, without prying eyes. When the fire had taken he returned to where she was sitting and reached out a hand to help her up. This time she gazed directly into his eyes as she raised her hand and placed it in his. Xerxes then walked her to a couch that was closer to the fire, still holding her hand.

Esther was relaxed, and enjoying being so close to the king. She lowered herself onto the larger couch and then he joined her, a small distance separating them. They were, however, close enough for him to catch a whiff of her perfume. They sat in silence for a time, and let the gentle warmth of the fire envelop them. Each of them had a whirlwind of thoughts and emotions swirling inside. Esther suppressed her feelings for the king, strongly doubting that she would be chosen as the next queen. She felt that there had to be someone far more worthy than herself for this exalted rank. Xerxes, for his part, could not allow himself to give in too quickly to what he was feeling, as he first needed to be certain that she was *the* one.

12

THE GENTLE WHIRLWIND

Esther looked forward to every moment she spent with the king. She had by now lost count of the number of dinner dates they had had. On each one he had gone to great lengths to please her. She fondly remembered the one time he had asked for her company much earlier than usual and had taken her on a tour of the bush reserve that surrounded the palace. The green hideaway had many exotic trees, bushes, and ferns, and the beauty of it took Esther's breath away. The thick foliage made it feel cool after the harsh heat out in the open, and Xerxes had had many walking trails created in it. The path they took meandered beside a gurgling stream, crossing it at several points via charming wooden footbridges. Esther simply did not want to leave. She felt like she had entered a magical land.

'It is so lovely here,' she told the king, her voice soft and full of emotion.

Later they visited the palace gardens, where Xerxes recounted the origins of the various flowers and plants found there. Most had been gifted to him by nobles of neighbouring provinces, as they all knew of his love of gardening. Esther's admiration for the king increased even more. She loved the boyish, playful nature that he reserved just for her. She liked the way he pulled out her chair for her before a meal, and how he enjoyed picking things from her plate – and encouraged her to do the same from his.

Whilst each of them tried to stifle the feelings that were growing for the other, they failed to realise that they were slowly falling in love.

One day Xerxes invited Esther to meet someone special. She was curious as she had not met any of the king's relatives. She was by now familiar with most of the palace staff, but that was as far as it went. They had just been on another exploration of the gardens, and he had walked Esther to his stables, which were adjacent to the gardens. They were spacious, clean, and airy, with the aroma of the fresh bales of hay drifting through them. They housed many beautiful horses of different colour and size, and the king knew each of them by name. He stopped at several of the stalls and told her stories relating to each horse's background. After this he invited her to proceed outside to the nearby field, where he asked her to wait while he fetched some treats.

Esther walked out into the warm afternoon sun and gazed about her. She suddenly noticed, on the far side of the field, the beautiful white horse she had watched several times from the palace windows. As she moved closer to the wooden fence surrounding the field, she could not take her eyes off him. The shimmering white creature began walking towards where she stood; he then broke into a canter, stopping suddenly quite close to where she was. Esther reached out her hand and spoke soft endearments, inviting him to come closer. He did just that and, once they had become acquainted, even allowed her to reach up and run her hands through his mane. Esther was mesmerised by so much beauty in one horse. The majestic creature whinnied softly as she gently stroked him. This was a special moment for her – she had never touched anything as soft as his mane. She ran both her hands through the silky hair on each side of his neck, and he allowed her to stroke him, clearly enjoying the attention. She then leaned in and placed her head on his forehead, dearly wishing she could enter the paddock and be closer to him.

Xerxes emerged from the stables carrying a small bucket containing his horse's favourite snack: oats flavoured with honey. He was stopped in his tracks by the sight of Esther and the horse so close together. He was simply astounded, and he recalled just how hard he had worked to gain every inch of this horse's trust; it had taken quite some time, and had required much bribery with exotic treats before he had eventually built a bond with him. And now this wretched horse was getting cosy with Esther so soon after they had met! At that very moment, although he was not aware of it, something deep inside him shifted and gave way. He strode over to where they were, and swung the bucket inside the fence so that the horse could eat.

'I see you are already closely acquainted,' he said, smiling.

'Yes, we seem to have become good friends,' she replied. 'We have been eyeing each other through the window for quite a while now.' Esther's voice bubbled with excitement. 'He seems to trust me,' she added, looking at the king with surprise written all over her face.

'His name is Pegasus. I got him as a gift from one of the provinces,' said Xerxes. 'He was only one year old when he arrived. His mother died soon after his birth, leaving him with an inability to trust anyone.'

'Oh no,' said Esther, 'that is so sad. You poor thing,' she said as she gently stroked Pegasus with renewed love and understanding. She knew how painful it was to lose a parent, and be ripped away from everything you once held dear.

'He would not eat for days after he arrived,' continued Xerxes. 'He was clearly traumatised, so I spent a lot of time with him and used treats to gain his trust. He doesn't allow many people to get close to him; you must be special.' He added the last comment without thinking.

'He is a beauty, and has a very special story,' responded Esther, her voice thick with emotion as she contemplated Pegasus' journey.

How could he resist your pure, angelic soul? I am the fool for fighting so hard to resist you! Xerxes told himself. The king could sense that the intense emotions he had been feeling for Esther were starting to rise to the surface again. For the past couple of weeks he thought he had successfully shut them down, but now he suddenly felt disarmed. He wondered if it could be because he was so moved by seeing her bond so deeply with his most trusted horse. Up until now he had resisted rushing into a decision, but right then, in that moment, he could hold back no longer. Without saying a word, he drew closer to where she was standing and put his free arm around her shoulders. This was the closest he had ever been to her, and it felt so right. They stood like this for a while, not saying a word, just enjoying the beauty of it all. He eventually turned to Esther and gently tucked back a strand of hair that was lying across her face.

'I love you,' he said gently. 'I love you so very much.'

'I love you too,' was the only response she could make, deeply moved as she was by the look on his face.

Esther was full of love for the king. The sudden freedom to release the deep feelings she had been fighting so hard to ignore now stirred intense emotion within her, causing a tight knot to form in her chest. Xerxes drew Esther to himself and held her tightly and they stood like this for a long time just enjoying being close to one another. They eventually left Pegasus and retraced their steps back to the palace for dinner. All who saw the pair that evening recognised that they had finally let go of all pretence of formality and the distance that they had been trying so hard to keep up. Love had won the battle after all.

13
—

THE ENGAGEMENT

SOON AFTER THEIR DINNER, Xerxes sent a message to Hegai, requesting that he be allowed to ask Esther's family for her hand in marriage. He could not wait any longer; he wanted her sitting beside him as queen as soon as possible. Hegai was elated with this development – not that he hadn't seen it coming; it had just been a matter of time. Since her first date with the king, it had started to become quite apparent that she was his favourite. Their frequent dining together and subsequent chatting away late into the night had become the talk of the palace, and those who served the king commented on how much lighter and happier he now appeared.

Because Mordecai had asked Hegai not to reveal his relationship with Esther to the king, Hegai now advised Xerxes that Esther was an orphan. Upon hearing this, Xerxes decided to propose to her the following day, and he instructed Hegai to make sure that she looked her best for the special occasion.

The following evening Esther indeed looked like a dream. Her flowing teal gown had an elaborate bow on one side, and swept the floor as she walked. Her hair was parted in the middle and, held in place by ornamental hair pins, cascaded in waves down her back. Her light make-up, combined with the deep colour of her gown, made her glow even more than usual. She was so in love with the king that even the slightest glance from him caused her to blush deeply; she was giddy with love and happiness. The food prepared for them was delicious, but butterflies filled her stomach and she had almost no appetite. Xerxes ate nervously too, unsure how she would respond to his proposal.

As was usual after dinner, they proceeded into the lounge and sat before the fire. This time they sat close together, and Esther snuggled close to the king. They sat in silence, watching the flames dance before them. Xerxes then casually stood up and made his way to the fireplace, as if to check the flames. Esther felt cherished, knowing that he doted on her and had wanted to make sure she was warm enough. He briefly poked at the cheerfully-burning logs, and then replaced the poker back in its stand beside the fireplace. Discretely reaching behind one of the ornaments on the mantelpiece, he retrieved a small box. Esther caught sight of it, and wondered what might be inside. She watched the king walk back to the couch. Then, instead of sitting down, he lowered himself down until he was kneeling before her, his steady eyes not leaving her face. She immediately sat upright with concern, unsure what he was up to. She had absolutely no clue as to what was about to happen!

Xerxes continued looking directly into Esther's eyes, she returning his gaze with a look of surprise. He adored looking at her – it seemed at times like these that the whole world faded away and she was the only thing left. Flicking the box open, he removed an elegant ring with large diamonds embedded in it. It was beautiful, and sparkled in the warm light of the flickering flames.

'My life has completely changed since I met you. The happiness I feel is because I love you with all my heart. Would you accept this ring as a symbol of my love for you? I love you, Esther, and want to spend the rest of my life with you. Will you be my wife and the queen of this kingdom?' he asked, tenderly lifting her hand.

Esther was shocked, and her eyes widened as she looked at him, letting his words sink in. His brows were slightly puckered as he waited anxiously for her response.

'Yes, yes!' she eventually managed to babble, smiling and nodding her head with excitement and joy. 'I *will* marry you, Xerxes! I want to spend the rest of my life with you too!'

The king gently slid the elegant ring onto Esther's finger, and then held on to her hand. He stood up and, drawing her up beside him, gave her a long, loving hug. He was clearly relieved that she had accepted his proposal. He lifted the hand with the ring on it, and they both admired it. Esther had long slender fingers, and the ring fitted her perfectly. She felt so happy, and all she could think about was how she was going to spend the rest of her life with him. She was lost in the moment and did not want it to end. She lifted her hand again, and her ring sparkled in the dancing flames. She looked deep into Xerxes eyes, stroking the sides of his face with her hands.

'I love you, Xerxes!' was all she could manage to say.

He drew her even closer; he wanted to love, protect, and comfort her even more now. He eventually led her back to the couch, and this time they sat close together. He wrapped his arms around her, and she snuggled in close to him once again. They gazed into the glowing flames and the logs that burned in the fireplace. There was no one to interrupt them, as all the servants had retired for the night. The couple sat quietly for some moments, contemplating the commitment they had just made. Esther now realised the full magnitude of the situation – she was going to be the new queen!

'You have nothing to worry about,' Xerxes appeared to read her mind. 'You are going to make the best queen the world has ever seen.'

As the evening wound to a close, Xerxes escorted Esther back to her chambers. They walked slowly, hand in hand, two people deeply in love. They stopped outside her door, and he turned her to face him. Gently cupping her face in his big, strong hands and tilting it upwards, he placed a long and gentle kiss on her forehead, before she entered her room and closed the door behind her.

Xerxes walked slowly back to his own chambers with a smile lingering on his face. He could still feel the warmth and soft touch of her skin against his lips. He had butterflies in his stomach; he could not remember when he had last felt like this. For him, the greatest gift on this day was that Esther loved him. He had seen the love in her eyes, and had felt her heart pounding as he had hugged her. He wanted to shout with joy, to sing and dance; he wanted the whole world to know that he was in love and loved in return!

The next morning he was up at first light; he had a lot of things to take care of. Firstly he held a meeting with his elders, and updated them on the news of his engagement to Esther, thereby declaring the search for a new queen now finally over. Everyone was delighted with his choice, and there was much celebrating. He declared that she would be crowned queen early the following week, and that a banquet would be held in her honour. The preparations, invitations and minute details of this most auspicious occasion were delegated to a trusted team. In the meantime, he informed them, he would be absent for a few days; they were to make sure that everything was ready on his return. He did not elaborate on the nature of this leave, and no one dared ask any questions. He simply requested that the horses and carriage be made ready for a journey. He next had a brief meeting with the head chef, and assigned one of his aides to advise Esther to pack and ready herself for travel the next day.

14

JUST US

THE HORSES HAD BEEN brushed, and their coats gleamed in the sunlight. Pegasus was one of them, alongside another three of the finest, making a handsome team. Xerxes assisted Esther to the carriage, making sure she was seated comfortably before going around to the other side and sliding in beside her. He looked at her and fell in love all over again. She was wearing a wide-brimmed straw hat which cast a shadow over her eyes, and the ribbon on it matched her light, flowing dress. Her feet were adorned with strapped sandals, and she wore no make-up or jewellery. She smelled and looked like a fresh rose. Although she felt at ease sitting beside the king, the growing sense of excitement and anticipation was almost more than she could bear.

'Where are we going?' she asked.

'I'm taking you to one of my favourite places,' Xerxes smiled, a playful sense of mystery dancing in his eyes.

'Is anyone else going to join us?' she asked.

The king smiled again, but would say no more. Esther was mindful of the fact that she was experiencing the last of her days as a commoner, and that soon there would always be servants in attendance wherever she went. She watched with interest as the coachmen made sure that everything was secure, before heading off. It was just her and the king in the carriage, and two coachmen sitting up front and driving the horses. A second carriage laden with their supplies and a few servants followed. Soon they were going at a steady pace, and the gentle breeze blew Esther's hair over her shoulders. As far as Xerxes was concerned, this was all he wanted – to have his future wife all to himself for the next few beautiful days, and he intended making them the best ones of their lives.

They travelled on through the countryside, waving back at the people they passed on the way. Xerxes looked at Esther tenderly, admiring her beauty in the sunlight; he loved beautiful things, and she seemed even more perfect than a rose. His hand involuntarily brushed back a stray hair that lay across her face. Her skin felt soft and silky, and a fresh surge of love for her flooded his heart. He lifted her hand that was resting in her lap and kissed the back of it. She turned and gave him a dimpled smile, which always managed to disarm him, and he gently placed her hand on his knee; she clasped it, thrilled at being so close to him. They rode on, chatting casually about the many beautiful sights they were encountering.

Xerxes had requested that they take the scenic route, as he wanted to show off some of the natural beauty of his kingdom to Esther.

'Oh, my!' exclaimed Esther as they came to a bend in the road where they had a clear view of a large, winding river that flowed parallel to the road. 'Can we stop here?' she asked, excited by the beauty that surrounded them. 'I would like to take a closer look at the river.'

Xerxes rang the little bell, indicating for them to stop. The horses pulled to a halt and the coachmen jumped off and opened the doors. Xerxes went around to Esther's side and helped her down the step. Then, after requesting some refreshments for both them and the horses, he caught up with Esther, who had already started making her way down the trail that led to the riverbank. The water was a beautiful blue as it flowed gracefully on its course. The riverbank had a number of large boulders, and Xerxes and

Esther found one on which they could sit and take in all the beautiful scenery surrounding them.

'There must be a rapid or waterfall further down,' suggested Xerxes.

'Oh, really?' answered Esther, munching on some fruit.

'Yes, can you hear that roaring sound?' he continued.

'Oh yes, I hear it now. I hope we can catch a glimpse of it,' she responded. They sat there for a while longer, enjoying the warmth of the sun and the light breeze.

'This has been a good rest for both us and the horses, but I think we now had better continue on our way,' said Xerxes as he got up and helped Esther to her feet.

The next leg of their journey took them along many more scenic routes. Again she hazarded asking where they were going.

'We are almost there!' responded Xerxes, but wouldn't let on any further. He was enjoying the suspense.

Eventually a large dwelling came into view. It was tucked away down a side road, and they rode right up to it. Xerxes grinned and spread his arms wide. 'Welcome to my hideaway!' he announced.

It was easy to see why the king loved this private refuge. Esther wondered who maintained it, as the gardens looked lush and green. She could clearly make out a pathway from the house to the woods, and she wondered where it led. They remained in the carriage while the servants busied themselves with offloading their luggage and opening up; they only alighted once the main entrance was opened.

Esther walked into a medium-sized lounge that was filled with splendour; it felt very welcoming. This was quite different to the regal look of the palace, but was comfortable and inviting all the same. She continued feasting her eyes on her surrounds while Xerxes went out to give instructions to the head servant. She suddenly realised that she had not had time to see Hegai before leaving the palace, and was therefore uncertain as to what was expected of her during this time. She did not yet fully know all the royal protocols, and yet here she was holidaying on her own with the king!

As soon as the servants had refreshed their chambers, Xerxes offered to show Esther around the place. He first took her to the quarters that she and her chambermaids would be sharing. Her bedroom was huge, and had an imposing canopy bed decked with the finest satin and silk. She noticed that some of her cases had already been bought in. The bedroom adjacent to hers was for her maids. They then inspected the rest of the house; she was amazed by the luxury of it all. They finished off with a tour of the garden, and then returned to the house. By now it was just after midday, and their lunch had been laid out for them. As usual, the kitchen staff had gone over and beyond to please the royals, and the meal was a long and leisurely one – they had all the time in the world to enjoy the good food and each other's company.

After lunch Xerxes advised Esther to put on her hat and a more comfortable pair of shoes as they were going out to explore. They walked slowly, side by side, through the woods, with two servants carrying small backpacks tailing them at a respectful distance. Esther could hear rushing water ahead, but could not be sure if it was a rapid or a waterfall. Her curiosity was soon satisfied, as they came upon the most beautiful waterfall she had ever seen. It was breath-taking; water dropped down in sheets from rocks that lined an overhanging cliff, falling into a large clear-blue pool that sparkled invitingly. They stood there for a while admiring the view, before Xerxes skilfully guided her to a large, low rock on which they could sit with their feet dangling in the water. He then quickly removed his boots and rolled up his trousers; Esther watched with interest, unsure of what was expected of her.

'Here, put your hand on my shoulder and I will help you out of your sandals,' said Xerxes, kneeling before her. She complied, biting back a quick protest that was about to escape her lips. He promptly undid her sandals, and spread out a small rug taken from the backpack a servant had been carrying. 'Let's sit here for a while,' he said as he lowered himself onto the rug. 'The water should help cool us down a bit.' They sat by the waterfall for quite a while, enjoying the solitude, the birdsong and the peaceful cadence of falling water, and at that moment they were altogether content to be just where they were.

That evening Xerxes dismissed the kitchen staff, as he wanted to prepare dinner with Esther. He watched with interest as she assembled the meat for the oven.

'That looks really delicious,' he commented, as he awkwardly finished cutting up the vegetables. Cooking was not one of his strong suits, but he insisted on helping.

'I hope it tastes as good as it looks,' she responded. 'You have done an amazing job with those vegetables for someone who does not get much opportunity to be in a kitchen.'

'I learned through watching,' he divulged. 'I spent a lot of time in the kitchen whenever my father went away on his trips; the kitchen staff allowed me to help them.'

They sat down to enjoy their meal, and the conversation was light and cheerful. Esther was enjoying her time alone with the king, knowing that moments like these would be far and few between when they got back at the palace. There they would have servants waiting on them at every turn, and she would need to ask for permission to enter his presence; she understood and accepted the confines of royal protocol. She was amazed at how the wall of royal reserve had fallen from around him, so that instead of a king, an ordinary person now stood in his place. Moments ago he had been cutting up vegetables like a commoner, and she loved this side of him – one which only she was privileged to be witnessing.

During the day they went out exploring all that the nature surrounding the house had to offer. There was so much to do and they made good use of it. Their evenings were spent sitting before the fire, talking and sipping their favourite drinks. Much to Esther's amazement, one night Xerxes even roasted some nuts! Above all, the couple enjoyed being in each other's company and getting to know each other better.

Unbeknownst to Esther, each night while she slept the king left to meet with his chief adviser, who stayed with the other servants in lodgings a short distance away, the stables being located there too. Each afternoon this advisor rode from the palace and met with the king each night. These meetings normally took around two hours, after which Xerxes crept back to the house and retired to bed. The chief advisor would only return to the palace to relay the king's wishes early the next morning. Although he had delegated the responsibility for planning the marriage and subsequent coronation and banquet to others, he still needed daily updates so that he could be sure that nothing was being overlooked. He wanted his own immediate family, which was spread far and wide, and all the important dignitaries to be present for this event. Everything had to be just perfect for Esther, his soon-to-be-queen!

Xerxes was relieved that everything seemed to be shaping up just as he had wished, as he wanted everyone to have a memorable night. The chief advisor had reported that all the wining-and-dining details had been taken care of. The hall was said to be almost ready for the banquet; one section had already been set up for the banquet, while another was the inauguration space – where they would make their wedding vows and Esther her vow as queen.

Xerxes had tasked Hegai with the task of having a suitable gown made for Esther, one which would complement both the heirloom jewellery he planned to gift her with and the crown that would adorn her head. The seamstress working on the wedding gown had given the indication that she was almost done. Besides this, a top hairdresser and make-up artist had been engaged to assist Esther in getting ready for the event.

15

ESTHER'S EVENT

O N THEIR LAST MORNING, Esther could not shake off the anxiety she felt. Her get-away with the king had flown by, and they were soon to be heading back to the palace. She felt as if she was now in wonderland and about to return to the real world. The immenseness of her upcoming position weighed heavily on her. She was soon going to be queen, and that carried with it many responsibilities. Her subjects would be looking up to her, and she shuddered at this thought.

King Xerxes had also seemed a little distracted that morning. He insisted that they go for a swim after they finished breakfast; it was almost as if he wanted to re-live all they had done over the past few days, before they set off back to the palace. They had both so enjoyed their time at the waterfall, and he now wanted to experience it all over again.

The water was still a little cold when they got there, so they stood on the bank and enjoyed the beauty of the place. Xerxes could sense that Esther was tense, no doubt thinking about all that awaited for her at the palace.

'Come here, my love,' he said playfully, gently pulling her closer to him and wrapping his arms around her.

'It's almost time to go back to the palace,' whispered Esther, regret evident in her voice. She drew comfort from his nearness.

'Yes, my love, we will be heading back soon. I love you so much, and I don't want you to ever forget that,' said Xerxes in a hushed voice. 'I hope you have enjoyed our little getaway; I only wish it could last forever!'

'I will always cherish it,' replied Esther, flashing him one of her dazzling smiles. 'We should come back here often.'

'I promise!' responded Xerxes, lifting her hand and kissing the back of it, then turning it over and planting another one on her wrist. 'Come, we need to start heading back now,' he added, leading them back to the pathway.

The two were deeply in love, and reluctant to tear themselves away from this haven. Xerxes knew how busy his schedule would get, and how limited his time with Esther would be. At times he would need to travel on demanding missions, and would be gone for days; if she were to travel with him, her life might be put in danger. But he vowed in his heart always to make time for her. They made their way back to the house hand in hand, enjoying the tranquillity of the forest surrounding them.

'I am going to miss this place,' said Esther. 'But I am also ready to start working alongside you,' she added.

'The kingdom is going to be blessed to have you as its queen,' responded Xerxes with sincerity. He had arranged for their bags to be packed and loaded into the carriage whilst they were away, leaving only their travelling clothes out.

'You do think of everything!' laughed Esther when she saw that all they needed to do was to get changed for their journey.

'I try my best,' replied Xerxes, now in a jovial mood. He was feeling on top of the world because he had just received confirmation that everything was ready for their wedding ceremony, and for Esther's coronation and the subsequent banquet.

The couple sat together in the back of the carriage as they journeyed home to the palace.

'I have loved every moment of our time together over the last few days,' said Esther as she caressed the palm of Xerxes' hand.

'No more than I have, my love,' responded Xerxes. 'Life at the palace can get really busy,' he continued, 'but I promise always to make time for you.'

'It's a big change for me,' Esther voiced her thoughts. 'I am not even sure where I should start; how will I know what to do when I become queen?'

'You will see that you have nothing to worry about, my love; you will be given all the advice and support you could possibly need. Also, I will be there for you; all you need to do is say the word and I will do it for you.'

'I am sure you will,' whispered Esther, gently squeezing his hand, her fears now put to rest. 'You will have to teach me everything.'

'I have a home-coming banquet planned for you tonight,' announced Xerxes as their carriage rolled closer to the palace. 'I would like to introduce you to everyone.'

'Is that so?' she responded. 'I don't think I have anything appropriate to wear; surely I should look my best for it?'

'Do not worry about a thing,' said Xerxes, a mischievous twinkle in his eye. 'I have taken care of it all!'

As they approached the palace he instructed the driver to take the drive that led to a back entrance, as he wanted to accompany her to her chambers himself. They climbed the stairs in silence, Esther carrying only her handbag; Xerxes had insisted she leave everything else for the servants to bring up later.

'Well, here we are. How are you feeling now?' Xerxes asked as they entered her quarters.

'A little hungry,' she replied.

'I am starving!' he agreed. 'We did leave in a rush, didn't we? Let's see what we can find to eat in your dining room.'

'You think of everything!' Esther said again, smiling in amazement when she saw that the table had already been set for them. They sat down and enjoyed a late lunch together.

'I really must leave you now,' said Xerxes, making his way around the table to where she sat. He knelt before her and put his hands around her waist. 'I cannot wait to see you again tonight,' he declared. 'Everyone will be waiting to meet you. It's going to be a very special evening!' He had a twinkle in his eyes.

'I am sure it will be,' Esther stifled a yawn, quite unsuspecting as to what the evening might hold.

'Now you need to take a good rest; I will leave you, and someone will come for you when it is time.'

'How many guests are we expecting?' Esther asked cautiously.

'Oh, just the usual dignitaries,' Xerxes replied casually, hoping she would not become suspicious. 'Now, you rest and get your strength back, and I will see you later in the hall,' were his parting words.

Esther was roused from her nap by the sound of a knock on her bedroom door. She must have drifted off into a deep sleep, as the sun had almost gone down. She opened up to find her maid announcing that it was time for her to get ready for the banquet. She was relieved to see a familiar face.

'I will wait for you in your dressing room,' said the maid.

The journey back to the palace had been tiring, but her sleep had restored her somewhat. Esther was grateful for the bath full of warm water and the sweet-smelling bath salts. She was a little taken aback when she later entered her dressing room and found a small team waiting to help her get ready – there was the seamstress who had worked on her gown, a hairdresser, and someone to help with her makeup; her regular assistant was also there to help wherever needed.

The hairdresser was the first in line. She had strict instructions to keep Esther's hair away from the top of her head, as she was going to be wearing a crown. She brushed and pinned Esther's hair, and then worked carefully at creating waves and cascading curls.

The final hairstyle made her look beautiful and innocent. The make-up artist took over next, and worked on refining Esther's natural beauty. Now all that was left was for her to be dressed in her gown.

Suddenly there was a gentle knock at the door, and the maid who answered it was more than surprised to find that their guest was the king himself!

'Your Majesty! Please come in,' she said courteously. 'Esther is about to go into the dressing room. You will find her in the bedroom.' The maid stayed behind as Xerxes proceeded to where Esther was.

Esther was staring at herself in the big mirror on her dressing-table. She found it hard to believe that the person looking back at her was herself; she had undergone such a huge transformation. Xerxes caught a glimpse of her in the mirror as he walked in, and he caught his breath.

'You look gorgeous!' he said, at a loss for any other words. His face was flooded with affection for her.

'Thank you,' answered Esther, looking back at him in the big mirror. She was still in her silk dressing gown, and added apologetically, 'I am not finished dressing yet. Am I late?' She could see that Xerxes was smartly dressed in his royal army regalia. 'You look very handsome,' she complimented him, as she got up and straightened his heavy royal chain-of-office, which she had noticed was a little askew. 'Perfect!' she said, as she smoothed down the shoulders and front of his garment. 'I apologise for being in my dressing gown,' she added a little shyly. 'You should have let me know you were coming, and I would have made sure that I was dressed and ready.'

'Not at all, this is perfect. I wanted to catch you before you got dressed,' said Xerxes. 'I have something for you,' With this he reached into his pocket and drew out a long, slender box, and opened the lid. Inside was a simply-elegant diamond necklace with matching earrings. 'I want you to have this, and I would be honoured if you would wear it tonight.'

Esther looked at the stunning set in wonder, and she was overwhelmed.

'It's so beautiful,' she murmured as she gently traced her fingers over the necklace, hesitant to touch the precious stones. Xerxes lifted it out of the box and undid the clasp. Turning Esther around to face the mirror, he placed it tenderly around her slender neck.

'I could not wait for you to have this,' he said.

Esther studied her reflection in the mirror, and at that moment she realised where she had seen this jewellery before. It was the same set she had seen in the portrait that hung in the main lounge!

'Yes,' said Xerxes, noticing the recognition that had dawned on her face. 'This set has been passed down in my family for generations. I think it looks the best on you, though,' he added playfully.

Esther recalled how she had felt so intimidated by the portrait of his regal grandmother that hung in the lounge. She was amazed that Xerxes considered she even remotely compared to her.

'Someone will come and escort you to the hall,' he said as he slowly lifted her hand and placed a soft and lingering kiss on it. Then he reluctantly took his leave so that she could finish getting dressed.

Esther now completed the set by putting on the matching earrings, before going to the dressing-room to see her gown. It was starting to dawn on her that tonight's event was a bigger deal than Xerxes had let on. Only one garment was hanging there, and Esther's heart skipped a beat when she laid eyes on it. She could not quite determine whether it looked like a sophisticated ball gown or a wedding dress. Her hands instinctively went to her neck, feeling the precious jewels that lay there. *Xerxes,* she said under her breath, *what is going on here?*

The seamstress and her maid walked in as Esther was staring speechlessly at the dress. Mistaking the expression on her face for one of impatience, the seamstress moved quickly, removing the sheer cover. The gown underneath was made of soft, shimmering satin and was ivory in colour. The bodice had a scooped neckline and a lace motif, and the skirt was flared – so that it would swirl as it swept the floor. The maid helped Esther out of her dressing-gown and eased her into the starched underskirt that was there to shape her gown. The fabric of the gown was soft as it brushed against her skin. She felt like a princess as she stood there, the seamstress and her maid securing the laces that held everything together. The dress was an excellent fit – it clasped her slender waist and flowed out gently to the floor, making her look elegant. The pair fussed over her, adding the finishing touches and completing the ensemble by handing her an exquisite bouquet of fresh flowers.

A few moments later there was a knock on the door, indicating that it was time to go; an elaborately-dressed aide had come to walk her to the hall. By now she knew that this was not going to simply be dinner with the king and a few special guests, and her suspicions were confirmed when the aide invited her to sit briefly so that he could instruct her on the upcoming proceedings.

'The king has invited several important dignitaries, along with family and friends, to attend the banquet,' he started. Esther simply nodded. 'I will walk with you to the entrance of the hall, where Mordecai will be waiting for you.' Her face brightened a little as she realised that her uncle would be nearby. 'Mordecai will walk with you down the aisle and leave you with the king.'

An image of what the hall might look like immediately formed in Esther's mind, and she was thankful for the fresh bouquet, which she held on to a little more tightly in order to steady her shaking hands.

'You don't need to be afraid, as there will be someone there to guide you every step of the way,' the aide reassured her, sensing her anxiety. Esther simply nodded again, by this stage feeling completely out of her depth.

'The king asked me to give you this,' he then said, drawing out a small, folded piece of parchment from the leather folder he was carrying. 'We will leave for the hall as soon as you are ready.' He then left her to read the note in private.

Esther hurriedly opened the parchment, as she was filled with curiosity. She immediately recognised Xerxes sprawling handwriting and signature. There were only a few words written on a small card: 'I cannot wait any longer for you to be my wife and queen. I will see you at the end of the aisle,' was all it said. Esther managed to maintain her composure, despite the fact that her suspicions about the magnitude of the event had now been confirmed. She neatly rolled back the parchment, and placed it safely in a nearby drawer. She took one last look at herself in the mirror, drew a deep breath, and motioned to the aide that she was ready. She was calm and collected as she walked towards the hall. The events of that evening would be etched in her memory for the rest of her life.

A red carpet had been laid from her chambers to the entrance of the hall. It was lined on both sides with ornate pedestals holding lush bouquets of roses. She smiled to herself as she wondered when Xerxes had planned all of this.

As he stood at the end of the aisle, Xerxes was relieved that everything was going according to plan. The hall was filled with the smell of fresh roses – he had made sure that there would be many beautiful floral arrangements to adorn the place. He knew that Esther loved white roses best of all, so he had insisted that each bouquet include some of these. He had also seen to it that magnolias would be mixed in with the roses. He wanted everything to be just perfect for his beautiful bride and queen.

Heralding trumpets started blowing as Esther approached the entrance to the hall. She was relieved to see Mordecai waiting for her, just as the aide had said. He reached out his hand, and she clasped it with all her strength.

'You look very beautiful,' he said, giving her hand a gentle squeeze. 'I am so proud of you! Are you ready to walk to your king?' Esther could only nod. 'The musicians will start playing the national anthem, and we will walk slowly towards him,' explained Mordecai. 'I will then leave you with him and sit in the front row. I will be close by, so you do not need to worry.' Again Esther nodded her head; she had somehow lost her voice. This event was much bigger and infinitely more momentous than she could ever have imagined. She fixed her eyes on Xerxes as he stood waiting majestically for her to join him.

The musicians struck up the national anthem, and everyone in the hall stood up straight, their hands by their sides and their heads held high; this was a most important occasion for the kingdom. Xerxes fixed his eyes on Esther, his beautiful bride. He was smitten once again, and his face was a testament of love as he watched her inch closer and closer. She was all he could see – her hair tumbling in waves over her shoulders, and her stunning gown. As the eyes of his beautiful bride locked onto his, Xerxes wondered if he even deserved her at all. Stunned admiration was evident in the eyes of the guests as they feasted on her beauty as she slowly walked by. Xerxes was relieved to see that she appeared to be taking everything in her stride. *That's my girl!* he said to himself, with immense pride.

Esther eventually reached where Xerxes was, and now stood before him. She was relieved that she had not tripped, or done anything else to embarrass herself. She had simply walked calmly down the aisle, her hand through Mordecai's arm; she was grateful to have had him close, as she felt way out of her depth. No one would have suspected the nervousness in her as she had returned smiles to the guests as she walked past them. There were so many of them there, and she again wondered when Xerxes had planned all of this.

She now stood facing her soon-to-be husband, Mordecai having retreated to the seat reserved for him. A soft smile quivered on Xerxes' lips as he looked at her. For a moment everyone in the hall seemed to have disappeared – all he could see was her. A golden glow appeared to shimmer around her, making her features appear softer and even more beautiful than ever. The look on his face said it all.

'You look so beautiful, my love,' he whispered. Every fibre in his body wanted to reach out and draw her close to him, but now was not the time.

'We are gathered here for two very important events,' announced the minister in charge of the proceedings. 'This is a very auspicious occasion for our king, and for the kingdom at large,' he continued. 'First is the wedding of our King Xerxes to his bride Esther,' he announced. This was met with loud applause. 'We will all then witness the king crown Esther as our new queen,' continued the minister. This final piece of information was met with even more clapping and cheering.

The minister then took Xerxes and Esther through the marriage service. Esther's mind was in a whirlwind, and she stood as if mesmerised, her hands in Xerxes', listening to him repeating his wedding vows. He promised to love and cherish her as his royal wife and queen. The word 'queen' triggered some memories – she recalled how she had always deemed the other girls more suitable than herself. For a moment she trailed further back, recalling the passing of her parents, followed by her exile from the country of her birth. An involuntary sigh escaped from her lips, as she realised how far she had come.

Esther's attention now focussed and she repeated her own

vows. Xerxes presence, and the warm pressure of his hands holding hers, helped her believe that what was happening now was not a dream but in fact real!

'I present to you the bride and the groom,' announced the minister as soon as the wedding vows were over. This was met with much applause, reverberating throughout the hall.

The royal minister then summoned for the queen's crown to be brought forth, and the next stage of the proceedings began. The guests watched as he received the crown, displayed on a blue velvet cushion, and presented it to Xerxes, who executed a grand salute and accepted it. He then did a sharp four-point turn, which resulted in his facing Esther. It might not have been evident to others, but Esther could see her boyish Xerxes behind the military display.

'Will you, Esther, promise to uphold and serve the kingdom in good faith?' led Xerxes.

'I will,' responded Esther in a clear voice.

'I now place this crown upon your head as a symbol of the authority that you carry as queen,' said Xerxes as he stepped forward and gently placed it on her. 'I also place this sword in your hand, as a symbol of protection for you and those in your kingdom,' he said, placing the white royal sword in her hand. 'You will overcome every attack of the enemy and come out victorious!' he concluded. He then extended his hand to her, inviting her to stand beside him. 'Ladies and gentlemen, I present to you your new Queen Esther!' he boomed.

The sound of trumpets blown in unison heralded the new queen. Esther had never felt so honoured in her whole life. She listened to the ecstatic applause, and her eyes misted with emotion. *Who am I to deserve of all of this?* she thought to herself. She wished that her parents could have been there to witness all that was happening in her life. Xerxes gently squeezed her hand, as he had felt the slight tremor in her grasp as the trumpets had started blasting.

As the royal couple returned to their seats a procession of guests filed forward to meet their new queen and pass on congratulatory messages to them both. First in line was Mordecai, who grasped Esther's outstretched hand, overcome with emotion. He looked deeply into Esther's eyes as he spoke with her, and Esther could clearly see the love and pride for her filled in them. Mordecai did not take too long with Esther, quickly moving on as he did not want to draw too much attention to himself.

Xerxes' heart was bursting with pride as he watched Esther winning the hearts of the people presented to her. She managed to speak with all the dignitaries who came up to give their congratulations. She responded with natural grace, expressing gratitude at their coming to share the special day, and acknowledging their generous wedding gifts, which had been brought in and put on display. Her apparent genuine interest in each of them made it easy for them to accept and love her. She listened to each guest with interest, noting all they had to say about the jobs they were doing; she was so looking forward to serving the kingdom alongside the king. Xerxes was delighted that he had chosen so well.

There was much celebrating at the wedding banquet that night. After the extended meal Esther and Xerxes stood up for their first dance as king and queen. She moved into his arms as if she was coming home. The couple whispered in each other's ears all through the dance.

'I am proud of you, Queen Esther. You handled that really well,' whispered Xerxes.

'When did you plan all of this?' was the first question that came to Esther's mind.

'As you slept,' whispered back Xerxes, mischievously.

'As I slept?' Esther asked incredulously.

'Yes, at the house,' was Xerxes amused response. 'I slipped out each night after you went to bed; it was so easy.'

'I never suspected a thing!' responded Esther, mimicking defeat and snuggling closer to him. 'You are amazing, and thank you for going to all this trouble,' she said.

'Anything for you, my queen,' he whispered back.

An announcement was eventually made that they would be taking their leave, but that the celebrations could continue throughout the night. Xerxes arose from his throne and extended his hand to Esther. They walked down the red carpet that had been laid out for them, leaving the banqueting hall to much applause and trumpet-blowing. They made a beautiful couple, and they looked so in love; it seemed everything had worked out perfectly for them. The royal couple then made their way, hand in hand, to the chambers that had been prepared for them for their first night together.

16

ESTHER'S JOURNEY BEGINS

THE FOLLOWING AFTERNOON A large carriage drawn by six white horses was waiting for the newly-wedded couple at the front entrance of the palace. The doors of the carriage were opened as soon as the coachmen saw them emerge. Xerxes helped Esther up the step, and she sank into the plush seat and waited for him to join her. The doors were closed, and they were on the way. Esther had no idea where they were going, but secretly hoped they were returning to the house near the waterfall; she had loved it there.

'Where are we going?' she eventually asked, unable to contain her curiosity any longer. She saw the mischievous look on the Xerxes' face, and suspected she would not receive an answer from her new husband.

'It's a surprise, my dear; have patience,' Xerxes responded with a twinkle in his eyes.

'Are we going back to the house by the waterfall?' Esther probed.

'Queen Esther, you need to have patience. Now hush, and enjoy the ride,' was all he would say.

Esther could not remember the exact route they had taken when they had travelled there, so she gave up trying to look for familiar landmarks. Instead she relaxed and enjoyed the ride, chatting happily with her new husband. Her mind was now able to begin to process the whirlwind of events that had taken place over the past few days. The thought that out of all the women

Xerxes had chosen to marry her, sent shivers down her spine, even more so now that she had been crowned queen. She had been profoundly moved by the coronation ceremony. The crown that had been placed on her head carried with it weighty expectations of duty, and she fervently prayed that she would be able to fulfil these. Although her life was changing beyond recognition, she was not deterred. She was ready for this next phase of her life, and determined to be a suitable helper for Xerxes.

Esther now remembered how she had found an opportunity to chat for a short while with her much-loved Mordecai at the coronation ceremony. Although the room had been full of people at the time, in that moment it had felt like nobody else was there besides the two of them. This day had been the fulfilment of the belief that Mordecai had had in her – that his Esther could one day become queen. She had not dared ask him how he had known this, but his ongoing unwavering love and support now instilled new confidence in her. She knew without a doubt that she had in him someone she could lean on when the going got tough. With that comforting thought in mind, she surrendered herself to the company of her husband and the amazing scenery they passed as their carriage rolled towards their destination. It finally came to a stop outside a wooden cabin. The coachmen quickly alighted, hurried to open the doors for them, and started offloading their luggage. There was not much to take in – just a couple of cases and some crates of food.

Esther was caught completely off guard when Xerxes lifted her off her feet and carried her over the threshold and into the cabin.

'Welcome to our home for the next few days,' he said, carrying her into the spacious lounge. There was a large fireplace in which a fire had already been lit, and the room was warm and inviting. She then set out to explore the cabin's layout; although it was small, it was well-appointed, and she felt comfortable and warm, and very much at home. Strolling back to the living area, she found Xerxes putting the last of the food items away.

'You must be exhausted,' he said gently.

'A little,' Esther admitted.

'Let me run you a bath,' he said. 'It will help relax you.' Xerxes had every intention of pampering his queen; he had requested that the servants leave them alone, and only be on standby. Esther wanted to object but, before she could do so, he swept her off her feet again and carried her to their bedroom. She was exhilarated, and let out a squeal of alarm. She wrapped her arms comfortably around his neck and snuggled against his chest. Xerxes put her down gently on the bed, and then went into the bathroom to fill the bath. He added some sweet-smelling bath salts to the running water, lit some candles, and dimmed the lights, so that a golden glow filled the room.

'Your bath is now ready, Your Royal Highness,' he announced in a playful manner. 'Would you care to come through, please?'

Esther walked slowly into the bathroom. Her pulse was racing, and she was still a little self-conscious around him. King Xerxes quickly noticed this, and continued in a jovial manner, hoping to put her at ease.

'Would Her Majesty like some help with her garments?' he asked. He turned her around so that she faced away from him, and undid the many laces at the back of her dress. He then helped her out of her garment, so that she stood before him in a silky under-garment that reached almost to her ankles. He gently kissed the back of her neck and whispered, 'Enjoy your bath, and take as long as you want. I will be preparing something special for this evening.'

Xerxes then headed for the lounge, where he went about pre-paring for their special night together. He ordered that a soft rug be laid in front of the fire, and candles be lit around the room. A tray of delicacies and some drink in gold goblets was set beside the rug. He then dismissed the servants, and settled down to wait for his bride.

He was lost in his thoughts when Esther emerged from her long bath. She had on a simple, light dress and had tied her hair in a bun, and she looked so naturally fresh and beautiful that his breath caught in his throat. He had never seen her look like this before, and he wondered if he would ever experience all of her. A sudden rush of love for her filled him, and he could not help but rise and walk towards her. A faint scent of her bathroom fragrances lingered around her, and he breathed in her sweetness. The look on his face made her feel loved and treasured. He guided her towards the rug and the warmth of the fire; she felt good and was very relaxed, especially after her therapeutic soak. They snacked on the delicious meal prepared for them, Xerxes enjoying feeding her special delicacies.

Xerxes sat with his back to the couch, Esther nestled in his arms. He could still catch a whiff of the bath salts she had used earlier. His sleeves were rolled up in a casual manner, showing off his strong hands, and she found herself stroking the hair on his arms. She found this relaxing, not realising how much he enjoyed it too. Xerxes gently placed his hand on Esther's forehead and stroked her hair. Then, having pulled off her hairband, it fell down over her shoulders, jet-black, glossy, and wavy. He gently turned her to face him, and for a moment she wondered if she would ever be good enough for him. But all these insecurities vanished when she saw the all-too-familiar look in his eyes. His face had taken on a softer and more relaxed demeanour; she had noticed this transformation whenever he looked at her. Esther hoped in her heart of hearts that there would never come a time when he would look at her with indifference. They enjoyed the comfort of the cosy fire for quite a while longer, and retired as the last of the logs had burned down and the embers were dying out.

The next morning Xerxes was the first to rouse from a long, deep sleep. Esther was still fast asleep, her cheeks a little flushed, and she looked peaceful and serene. He gazed tenderly at her, and fell in love all over again. It was almost like looking at a sleeping baby, only this was his Sleeping Beauty. He had no intention of waking her, so he slowly and quietly slid out from under the covers, threw on his morning gown, and quickly left the bedroom. He headed towards the kitchen to order some breakfast for him and his queen. The kitchen staff were suddenly all busy pressing grapes for juice, and placing whole grapes in one bowl and fresh bread in another. In no time the king and queens' breakfast tray was ready. In the meantime Xerxes slipped outside into the garden and selected a single white rose, which he placed diagonally across the tray that had been left per instruction at the entrance to their chambers.

When Xerxes next walked back into their chambers, he brought a tray laden with their breakfast. Esther was sitting up in bed.

'I should have done that,' she protested.

'Not in this house,' Xerxes playfully responded. 'I am going to be waiting on you, Your Royal Highness.'

Esther's eyes had been drawn to the perfect rose that lay on the tray, and she now picked it up.

'This is so beautiful,' she said. 'Thank you.'

'I thought you would like it,' replied Xerxes. 'But I still think that *you* are the most beautiful flower of all,' he said, a fresh surge of love for her washing over him. They were completely at ease with each other as they enjoyed their breakfast together. They were in no rush – they had the next few days all to themselves.

The cabin Xerxes had chosen for their honeymoon was tucked away beside a lake, and had a small but charming garden which added to the natural beauty of the place. There was a cocoon-shaped swing chair on the porch, and they spent a lot of their time sitting in it and taking in the beautiful, peaceful views of the lake and beyond. Far away from the madding crowd, they were in a world of their own, one where time did not exist. Sometimes they ventured down to the lake, where they took long swims in the crystal-clear water, and once or twice even tried their hand at some fishing. They also took long walks along the winding lake shore, exploring and then finding sunny nooks where they could roll out their mat and towels and bask in the warmth of the afternoon sun.

Esther had never felt so treasured and loved in her whole life. She glowed from the experience, and Xerxes was astounded at how she appeared to be growing even more beautiful. He reflected that his wife was not only beautiful, but also humble, charming and cheerful. She had a joyful spirit, which enriched him. He now could not imagine life without her. He wanted to please her at all times, and was willing to give her anything her heart desired – she just had to name it. He was deeply in love with her.

News about Esther's marriage to the King and subsequent coronation spread fast, and was the talk of town. The fact that no one appeared to know which province she hailed from only served to make it just a little bit more sensational, with everyone trying to source a bit of information about her.

'I heard our new queen is of incomparable beauty,' said one woman as she drew water at the well.

'Yes,' answered another,' I have it on good authority that she is absolutely gorgeous and that the king could not resist her.'

'Do you know which province she is from?' asked the first woman cautiously, taking a pause from the strenuous hoisting of her now-full bucket.

'I do not think I have heard it said where she hails from,' the second replied.

'That is very puzzling,' the first woman responded. 'If she were from our province, we would be shouting it from the mountaintops, letting people know that the she was one of us.'

'Yes,' agreed the second woman, laughing. 'We would be bragging about how *we* had made it into royalty!'

They ended up concluding that Esther's identity was probably being kept secret in order to protect her from people who would seek favours because they came from the same province as her.

17

Esther's New Life

Esther quickly adjusted to her new life in the palace, taking on her role as queen with enthusiasm. The first few weeks were spent redecorating their royal chambers to her own taste. Xerxes had had them stripped, not wanting anything left to remind him of his bitter disappointment over Vashti.

'I have a confession to make,' said Xerxes on the day they arrived back from their honeymoon, a sheepish look on his face.

'Is the bed not made?' Esther joked, as he fumbled with the keys to the royal chambers. She had never seen him so hesitant before, and wondered what lay on the other side of the door.

'Welcome to the royal chambers,' he announced stiffly as it swung open.

It was plain to see why he had been hesitant – the place was mostly unfurnished; the walls were unpainted, and the drapes had been taken down from most of the windows.

'Well, well, well,' said Esther in utter confusion. 'What happened in here?'

'I ordered everything to be taken down when Vashti left,' he answered, a defeated tone in his voice. 'I just never got the inspiration to put it back together again.'

'Oh, I see,' said Esther, a little taken aback by this revelation, and uncertain how to respond. 'I am so sorry, Xerxes. I know that you were hurt badly,' she said quietly. 'I have not had much experi-

102

ence with this, but I would love to try to re-decorate it for you,' she offered hesitantly.

'I wouldn't have anyone else do it,' responded Xerxes, much relief in his tone.

'We will see if I can match your creativity!' smiled Esther, quite warming to the idea of furnishing the royal chambers to her taste.

'Here, let me show you around, not that there is much to show off,' laughed Xerxes, taking her by the hand. He then took her on a brief tour of the royal bedroom, the lounge, the occasional rooms, the private kitchen and the huge balcony that extended from the chambers.

Everything was of magnificent proportions, and Esther's head started filling with ideas of how to make it look both elegant and comfortable. She knew a lot about furniture, having often accompanied her father on the delivery of his hand-crafted creations to fine houses. She immediately started creating a plan for the restoration of the royal chambers, and she soon had in mind just which fittings and furnishings would best suit their new home.

Esther was held in high esteem by everyone. King Xerxes allowed her to make her mark, and as a result her presence was felt and was well received in all four corners of the kingdom. She especially reached out to widows and orphans; she became mother, encourager and advisor to many of them, and she went to great lengths to ensure their needs were met. She worked in many other arenas as well, and managed to attend most of the functions she was invited to. She did not pretend to know everything, and she always managed to leave people feeling filled with hope and encouragement. And so she grew in the hearts of all the people.

Most evenings the royal couple sat together in the study above the lounge. They would relax before the fire, and chat away late into the night. It was in these moments that Esther poured out her heart to the king about matters she was facing, and he in turn shared with her the issues he was dealing with. Here they encouraged and gave advice to each other.

Esther was extremely proud of Xerxes' achievements. She was his biggest fan, and he could see her admiration of him glowing in her eyes. This always spurred him on to do better, and to make her even more proud of him. He was similarly proud of her and the good work she was doing. He loved how passionately she carried out her duties. She took no instructions from anyone, and yet she kept going and kept busy. She did not have to do all this – after all, she was the queen. She could have remained in the palace, spending her time walking in the gardens, inviting other women for drinks, and showing off her many gowns. But she was different – her heart for her people was too big for her not to get involved in their lives.

18

THE THREAT

Esther and Mordecai still maintained their close relationship after her marriage and coronation, and he visited the palace regularly. Their bond remained strong, and she looked forward to his visits, when they would sit and exchange stories. He brought news from the community, and she shared tales from within the palace walls and further afield. Mordecai enjoyed hearing about the programmes Esther was carrying out. He listened with wonder at all the initiatives she was involved in, and was amazed at how far she had come and all that she had achieved in such a short space of time. He wished her parents could be there to see the strong and influential woman she had become. He knew she carried a heavy burden as queen, but he believed that she was capable of handling everything that came across her path.

One day Mordecai was not his usual inquisitive self; his heart was heavy and he carried some disturbing news. He had overheard two royal officials plotting to assassinate the king. He was still trying to work out how to share this delicate but crucial information with Esther. He knew how deeply she loved Xerxes, and he was not sure how she was going to react when she learnt that his life was in danger. Mordecai's mind was elsewhere as he sat listening to Esther's news, and she quickly noticed that he appeared distracted.

'Is everything all right, Uncle?' Esther ventured. 'I hope I am not boring you with my stories. You appear distracted.'

'Not at all, my dear,' Mordecai answered. 'I have just had a very long day, and as you know I am not young anymore.' They both laughed at this statement, as he resented being called 'old' by anyone. Esther knew how private he could be, and accepted that she might never learn what was troubling him.

Just how private Mordecai could be was evident from the way he had insisted that Esther not divulge her ethnic background to the king. He had insisted she follow these instructions.

'I know you don't agree with me on this, Esther,' he had told her, 'but I have my reasons. You do trust me, don't you?' Esther had eventually stopped challenging him on this issue. Mordecai was not only private but also obstinate, seldom changing his mind about things.

So, rather than pressing Mordecai to share his concerns with her there and then, she busied herself by pouring a drink and slicing some cake for him. She placed these on the side table next to where he was sitting.

'Thank you, my dear,' he said, smiling affectionately at her. Esther then poured a cup for herself, and helped herself to a slice of cake. They enjoyed their refreshments for a while in silence. Unlike their previous visits, when they had caught up on what had happened since they last had met, this time they were lost in their own thoughts.

Mordecai put down the cup he had been cradling in his hands. He had hardly drunk anything at all. He looked directly at Esther, with a sombre expression on his face.

'The king's life is in danger,' he said, choosing not to beat around the bush.

'Are we under attack?' was Esther's swift response, assuming the whole kingdom was in danger.

'No, it is not the whole kingdom that's in danger,' Mordecai replied. 'The threat is only to the king.'

'From whom?' Esther asked in disbelief. She found it incomprehensible that anyone would want to harm her husband. A sudden feeling of dread came over her, and her hands began to shake.

Mordecai could see that the news had shocked her, but he knew he had to warn her so she could alert the king. He went on to give her the exact details of the plot to assassinate king Xerxes.

'It was by mere chance that I overheard the two men conspiring to commit this heinous crime. They are not aware that I had overheard them.' Esther leaned forward in her chair, her heart pounding with concern for not only Xerxes but Mordecai as well. 'There is no way they could have known I was in the room,' he added, as if reading her thoughts.

Mordecai proceeded to give Esther an account of how he had learned this vital information. The two officials, Bigthan and Teresh, had hatched their plan to assassinate the king during one of their long afternoon lunch breaks, the time most of them who were not on duty would go back home to have a meal and freshen up. Mordecai had not returned home that day, but instead had retreated to a secluded office in order to meditate and pray in silence. This was a habit he had developed over the years, and this was one of many secluded spots he visited during his lunch breaks. This time the room he had been in was adjacent to a large, open courtyard which had benches along the walls, where people could sit and chat in the shade. No one ever paid any attention to Mordecai's routine, nor showed any interest in what he did, as he was deemed to be 'different'. He would normally have been alone; but not on that day.

Presently he had heard footsteps of people entering the courtyard. His curiosity had been aroused, as usually no one came to that part during that time of day. Bigthan and Teresh had then sat down directly outside the room he was in; they had clearly chosen this spot as they had wanted to make sure they had a full view of the courtyard so that they could easily have seen if anyone had came their way. They had had important issues to discuss, where no one could hear them.

Unbeknownst to them, Mordecai had been just on the other side of the wall against which they were resting their backs. It had been evident that they had been about to have their afternoon meal, as the strong smell of cooked food floated his way. Mordecai had wondered who had joined him out there that afternoon, as he would normally have been alone. He had wondered what important matters they might have been wanting to discuss, away from all their colleagues. Their voices had carried well, and he had heard everything they had discussed, without any trouble at all. He had been horrified when he had discerned that the two of them were hatching a plot to assassinate the king. They had been, unwittingly, within his earshot, and they had sounded very confident that their plan would succeed.

'This is no small matter, Esther,' Mordecai told his niece, leaning forward in his chair after finishing his account. 'They are going to carry out their plan in the next few days.'

'But the king will be safe if he moves quickly to stop these traitors, ' she said. Esther's heart pounded at the thought of her husband being in danger.

'Yes,' agreed Mordecai. 'It is a good thing we know their plans. You must warn the king immediately, so that he can quickly expose and punish them.'

A stab of pain seared through Esther's heart; she could not imagine anyone wanting to harm the king. She had cringed in horror as she listened to Mordecai relate what the two were plotting to do. She resolved to make a report to the king as soon as possible, so that these traitors could not only be stopped before they did any harm, but also be prosecuted for treason.

'They will not get away with this,' Esther fumed, to no one in particular. She was so agitated that she could barely taste the sweet drink she was sipping. Mordecai took his leave of her earlier than usual, so as to give her time to prepare herself for talking to the king.

'Please be careful,' he urged as he left. He was greatly unsettled because of the threat to her husband's life.

That evening the king had a dinner engagement with some of his dignitaries. Esther had excused herself, knowing the meeting would take an extended period of time. Whenever the king was detained in this way, she usually dined alone in the library, which overlooked the lounge and main dining room. She always looked forward to his coming up to join her as soon as his dinner engagement was over. This night the palace staff had made the library warm and cosy for her. As always, wanting to please her, they had brought up a large tray laden with her favourite dishes. She dished up a plate, poured herself a drink and, feeling cold, took a seat close to the fire. She ate in silence, not paying much attention to what was on her plate. Her mind was in a turmoil. Mordecai's news of the assassination plot had thrown her into fear. She fervently prayed that the king would overcome this threat to his life and leadership, and that he would come to no harm.

Esther leapt out of her chair when she heard the king's footsteps coming up the stairs. She could hardly wait for him to come through the door, and rushed to throw herself into his arms. Thoughts of treachery had plagued her mind because he had arrived a little later than usual. Xerxes was a little alarmed at this intense gesture.

'What is the matter? Are you okay?' he gently asked her.

'I thought I might never see you again,' Esther answered in a quivering voice. 'You are late.'

'I was just downstairs,' he jokingly protested, having no idea of the gravity of the situation. 'You know how our meetings are.' He wondered what she meant by 'I thought I might never see you again'; he imagined he must have heard her incorrectly.

Xerxes poured them both something to drink; he knew Esther liked honey and ginger, not that she minded having a goblet of wine if he were joining her. He then steered her to their normal seat by the fire. As she sank into the couch he sensed her tension, and immediately went and stood behind her and began to rub her shoulders. He could feel how tense she was.

'What has happened that you are in such a state, my dear?' he asked. 'Whatever it is, it can be resolved. You know I can take care of anything,' he added jokingly. He continued to rub her shoulders, trying to encourage her to relax.

Esther tilted her head backwards and looked up at him. Then she lifted her hands and placed them on his arms.

'Come and sit beside me,' she said. He stopped his massage, and sat down beside her, drawing her nearer.

'What's on your mind?' he tried again. 'It seems like you have had quite the day. What can I do to make it better?' He had never known Esther to panic, and alarm bells had started ringing in his head. He could not imagine what might have caused her to get into such a state.

'How was your day?' she asked, trying to find a way to break the news to him.

'You tell me what is on your mind first,' he prodded gently, rubbing her wrists. Her hands felt cold under his touch, despite the generous warmth coming from the fireplace. He became more alarmed when she broke down in sobs. 'What's the matter, Esther?' he said. 'I am here now; we can work through this, I promise.'

Esther had been carrying the heavy burden of knowledge all afternoon, and the sight of Xerxes had caused her emotions to overflow out of control. Her sobbing made her develop a small hiccup. He gently disengaged from her and went over to the side table to pour her a cup of water.

'Here, drink this,' he said, handing her the cup. 'It should help.'

Esther took a sip and tried to get her hiccups under control. 'You need to tell me what this is all about,' he continued. 'We can work through it together.' She eventually calmed down enough to tell him about the threat to his life.

It was now Xerxes' turn to be alarmed, and to say he was livid would be an understatement. His face blanched; it incensed him these rogues were planning to undo all the progress he had made in establishing peace in this once-turbulent kingdom. Despite the rage that churned inside him, he lovingly cupped Esther's face in his hands, gently lifting her chin and looking deeply into her eyes.

'I will take care of this,' he vowed. 'Don't worry yourself about it. Nothing is going to happen to me.'

New tears formed in Esther's eyes as she saw the love in his face. Even at that moment of uncertainty, she believed him; she knew that he would deal with it. And all the tension in her body eased under his gentle touch.

'Please, promise me you will be careful,' she murmured. He replied by wrapping her in a great big hug. He planned to leave no stone unturned in bringing the two culprits to justice.

Now that Esther was so much calmer, she managed to briefly update him on all the other events of her remarkably busy day. Xerxes felt relieved, and enjoyed hearing all that she had been up to. He loved it that she took on so many projects, and how involved she had become with various different groups in the kingdom. He now listened with amazement as she told him about a farming project she was trying to put together with a group of widows who had approached her seeking help. Her heart was intent on finding ways to make life better for everyone around her.

The threat to the king's life had caught Esther off guard, and she wondered if there were more enemies in the kingdom, over and above these two traitors. It was a bitter pill to swallow, and she found herself putting up subconscious walls of precaution and protection where she once had proceeded with abandonment. She knew first-hand how much her husband had invested in ensuring that peace and justice prevailed in the kingdom. Xerxes was a highly-intelligent man, one who had a way of simplifying complicated and confusing situations so that they became quantifiable and manageable. She thought back to what he had told her about the countless sacrifices he made in order to ensure that livelihoods remained secure and the economy buoyant. The low-burning fire continued to envelop the room in warmth as they sat enjoying each other's company, away from the prying eyes of others.

Esther woke from a restless sleep to the scent of fresh roses. She had tossed and turned for most of the night, and had only drifted off to sleep in the early hours of the morning. She knew Xerxes too had lain awake for the better part of the night; she could tell from his breathing that he had not been asleep. The rise and fall of his chest had eventually lulled her to sleep, but he had lain awake longer, his mind racing. He could not wait for the break of day to arrive, so that he could launch his plan. He would stop at nothing to bring the culprits to justice. He had crept out of bed at the first light of dawn and, knowing how much Esther loved white roses, had picked her a single, perfect bloom. As he walked back into the bedroom, he was relieved to find her still sound asleep. He knew she had had a hard night. He laid the single flower on top of his pillow – so that she would see it as soon as she opened her eyes.

Xerxes met with his counsellors and apprised them on the threat that had been made to his life. They immediately called on Mordecai to give them a detailed account, and everything he reported was recorded in the royal journals, together with their plan of action. The counsellors acted swiftly, and it did not take long to bring the two culprits to justice.

Both Mordecai and the king were excused from the room

when Bigthun and Teresh were summoned for questioning. Unsuspecting of their imminent demise, these two traitors strode in with confidence. They had no idea that their secret plan had been uncovered, and that were about to face the full wrath of the law. But the evidence against them was overwhelming, and they ended up confessing. They were taken out of the room bound in chains, and escorted to a dungeon from which no one had ever made it out alive. Justice had been swiftly carried out, and the kingdom was now rid of the threat that had been hanging over the king's head.

Esther was grateful for the part Mordecai had played in saving the king's life, and pleased that his name appeared in the king's journals. She was also relieved that the traitors had been exposed and dealt with, and that they were no longer a threat.

19

Haman and a New Threat

As the dust settled on the assassination attempt, Xerxes decided he needed to further secure his safety. He resolved to do this by having a major reshuffle of his officials. Amongst his employees was one ambitious officer named Haman.

Haman was tall and had the build of a warrior. The fact that he was a head taller than most others made him feel that he was better than everyone else. He was supremely confident, and driven to succeed at all costs and to the highest level he could. On top of this, he was very outspoken, and took every opportunity he could to offer his opinion on all matters. Nothing went unnoticed under his watch, and he had a solution for every problem. Because he caused a stir wherever he went, he caught the king's attention early on. Haman displayed the very qualities he admired, so he had elevated him to the highest office, without even first consulting any of his advisors. Thus Xerxes promoted him to the powerful position of 'Overseer of the Nobles and Officers'. Xerxes had firmly believed that he was the man for the job, as he was fearless in taking charge. So Haman was now second-in-command to the king.

Haman consequently hosted a very large party to celebrate his promotion. He made certain that everyone knew that he was second only to the king. After bidding farewell to the last of their guests, he and his wife Zeresh were satisfied that the celebration had gone well, and that it had further cemented his position amongst his peers.

'The night was a success!' declared Zeresh as they walked back into their living room.

'It most certainly was,' replied Haman. 'And with good reason! Excellent food, excellent wine – fit for one second only to the king!'

'Did you see the admiration in their eyes?' asked Zeresh as they settled down, each with a drink in their hands.

'Yes. They all know that I am in a position of power, and that their very lives depend on me.'

'Yes, indeed!' egged on Zeresh. 'You are almost equal to the king.'

'Well, I *am* equal to the king,' Haman answered back cockily. 'The king himself does not make any decisions without asking my opinion first.'

'You are mighty in power, Haman. You should therefore be treated just like the king,' declared Zeresh. 'Now,' she continued, stifling a yawn, 'It has been a long day and I am really tired. I am going up to bed. Coming?'

'I will join you soon,' replied Haman, remaining seated and deep in thought.

His wife's statements played over in his head. *I am equal to the king*, he thought. *I should be treated just like the king*. Then it came to him, *Everyone should bow down to me just as they do to the king. I will make a point of suggesting this to him tomorrow*. Satisfied with his resolution, Haman retired to bed.

The king's decree requiring everyone in the kingdom to bow down to Haman was issued the following day, effective immediately. Haman had not even had to justify his request; the king had granted it without a second thought. Haman had always secretly admired how all the officials bowed in reverence the king, and he was now delighted to be accorded the same reverence. His ego was given a boost each time the king consulted him on matters of the kingdom, and now his heart swelled with pride when the officials deferred to him and the people showed him the honour he believed he deserved. They prostrated themselves before him whenever he came into view. No one dared to defy the king's decree.

Word soon filtered through to Haman that there was someone who was not obeying this command. He had been alerted to it by some of the officers at the king's gate. Deciding to investigate this disobedience, he passed by the palace gates and saw for himself that this was indeed true – one man remained standing in his presence. Haman was infuriated by this disobedience, and committed himself to finding a way to punish the offender.

Mordecai was amongst the king's officials at the gate, but he held different beliefs to everyone else. He refused to bow down before Haman whenever he passed by. His colleagues at the gate cautioned him about this, and pleaded with him to obey the new command.

'I will not bow down to anyone as it goes against my beliefs as a Jew,' declared Mordecai, standing his ground firmly. 'I am ready to face the consequences,' he added firmly.

Unbeknownst to him, the very same men who had been urging him to comply were the ones who had then informed on him. They were keen to see how Haman was going to handle Mordecai.

'He has brought this upon himself,' they agreed amongst themselves. 'He could be locked in the dungeon and the key thrown away; he should reconsider before this happens. He will live to regret it!'

Haman summoned Mordecai to his office at the palace; his intention was to single him out away from his peers. When Mordecai knocked at his door, he was sitting in the oversized chair that he had designed to mimic the king's throne.

'Enter!' Haman boomed, when he spied him at the entrance. He stared at Mordecai as he walked across the room towards him, waiting for him to bow down before speaking to him, as was expected. Mordecai, however, made no attempt to do so, and instead remained standing tall while he greeted him.

'You wanted to see me?' asked Mordecai, unaware that Haman was barely able to conceal his rage at the lack of respect being shown him.

'I have it on good authority that you are in defiance of a law issued by decree of the king,' declared Haman in an icy tone, coming straight to the point. Mordecai stood calmly before him, noticing the latter's tightly-clenched jawline and significantly-lowered eyebrows.

'I have heard of the command you are referring to,' said Mordecai. 'You must not interpret my not bowing to you, or anyone else for that matter, as a sign of disrespect; it simply goes against my beliefs. I hope you can understand that.' Then, in a tone that gave no opportunity for negotiation, he added, 'The king can continue to count on me to carry out my duties to the highest standard. If there is nothing further, I will return to my post and relieve my colleague.'

'You can go back to your post,' growled Haman, realising that he was not going to get any satisfaction from him. He had seen the look of calm resolve on Mordecai's face, and how he held himself confidently erect. In his imagination he had seen him apologising profusely, begging for forgiveness, and then promising to start complying. Now Mordecai's calm, resolute response caused a fresh surge of outrage to course through his veins. *The man does not fear me! I will show him who is in command!* His mind was in a frenzy as he sought to take revenge.

Haman soon discovered that Mordecai was a Jew, one of a race of people dispersed throughout the kingdom. Thinking he might face similar defiance from all of them, he resolved to take care of this defiant behaviour before it spread. *I will not sit back and allow the kingdom to be taken over by a bunch of rebels!* He did not go immediately to the king with his concerns about this potential threat, but instead formed a plan of his own to deal forcefully with the insurgents. He would not rest until he had accomplished his mission.

Haman soon found the perfect opportunity to put his plan into action. The king had called him in for a meeting, and had asked if there was anything on his mind. Haman avoided mentioning Mordecai by name at this stage, as he wanted to make it appear that the problem was widespread and quickly getting out of control. He immediately informed him about the Jews, a people who had a different religion and who were settled throughout the kingdom. These outsiders had the potential to cause disunity as they had a totally different belief system. He skilfully recounted how these people were increasing in number and acting in disobedience to decrees that had the seal of the king's ring on them. Haman not only apprised the king of this situation, but went on to offer a solution. He urged him not to tolerate this disobedience within his kingdom, reminding him of other cases of disobedience that had posed a threat in the past, and how they had been dealt with.

King Xerxes valued the hard-won peace in his kingdom, and saw merit in what Haman was presenting. He was well-satisfied with this proposal, and gave him permission to punish the people concerned and do all that was necessary to restore order and unity. Haman, emboldened by the king's support, offered to use his own money to carry out his plan to rid the kingdom of this unruly mob. However the king refused his money, deeming the project 'kingdom business' and therefore a matter for the palace.

Haman wasted no time in setting a date when this punishment would be enforced. He prepared a new decree for all the districts, and had it translated into all the various languages – so that everyone would understand exactly what the consequences of civil disobedience would be. The king's signet ring had been entrusted to him, and he used it to full advantage, officially signing this new decree in the king's name and sealing it with his ring. No one would dare defy him this time!

Haman's new decree dripped with blood, sending chills down the spines of all who heard it read out. On a single day, the thirteenth day of the twelfth month, all who defied this order that Haman be honoured, and all who belonged to them, would be killed. A dark cloud of despair hung over the Jews; entire cities throughout the kingdom were horrified by this edict.

Mordecai was devastated when he read the decree. He was so overwhelmed that he tore his clothes, dressed in sackcloth and sprinkled dust and ashes over himself – as a sign of mourning. The fact that he had been the trigger for this dire turn of events caused him even more anguish, and the burden weighed heavily on him.

He walked to the city wall, wailing loudly and bitterly; he wanted the whole kingdom to be aware that he was in a deep state of grief. He could not enter the city because no one dressed in sackcloth was allowed through the gates. He was not alone in his mourning – every time the edict was read it was followed by the sound of wailing, as terror struck the hearts of the Jews. Dread and hopelessness hung over their homes; there seemed to be no way out, since it had been signed and sealed in the name of the king. They had nowhere to go to escape the approaching slaughter. The dread weighed most heavily on Mordecai, as he knew that his actions had been the cause of it. He sat at the city gates and wept bitterly. He was in great distress and turmoil; no one could comfort or console him.

Life in the once-vibrant Jewish neighbourhoods changed in an instant. The noisy market places and children's playgrounds were now silent. People's first instinct was to hide from the fast-approaching doom, and they ventured out only to get the bare necessities; they felt safer inside behind bolted doors. Their livestock was now kept in stalls, rather than being allowed to roam the fields. The wells, where the women used to spend time sharing news of the community, were now deserted; instead they drew their water quickly and silently, and then headed straight back home.

A solitary figure hurried down a deserted road, carrying a heavy load on his shoulders. He eventually turned in at one of the houses, and tapped quietly on the door. The sound of chains rattling and bolts being drawn back accompanied the opening of the door.

'What took you so long?' asked the man anxiously, as he dropped his load on the floor.

'The new bolt securing the door was stuck,' answered his son, a young man possibly in his early twenties.

'Well, we need it to keep safe, so that is alright. We will get used to it soon,' advised his father. Two young children, a boy and a girl, rushed out from an adjacent room as soon as they heard his voice.

'Father, you are back!' they piped, clinging to his legs in excitement.

'Can we go out now and play close to the house?' begged the girl.

'It is hot and boring in here,' chimed in the boy. 'Why can't we go to the stream for a swim?'

'This will not last forever,' comforted their father. 'You will be back to playing outside with your friends soon.'

'When is soon, Father?' asked the older boy. 'We have been hiding away and doing nothing! For how long are we going to have to keep this up? It is unbearable! Why do we not demand to see the king or even fight to save ourselves? A group of us are willing to go out and seek justice; we cannot just sit back in silence anymore!' he pleaded, his temper beginning to rise.

'It is not time to do that yet, my son,' his father calmly responded. 'You are the oldest in this family, and must look after your mother and younger siblings whenever I am away. That is all you need to worry about for now. We will be advised on the appropriate action to take when the time comes. I have managed to find just enough food for us for the coming weeks. Trust our leaders, my son; they have never let us down before. They have walked with us and led us through adversity many times in the past. Trust them.'

20

THE CALLING

ESTHER WAS DISTRESSED BY the report she had just received from her trusted maid. 'I hear that Mordecai is covered from head to foot in dust and ashes,' she had said. 'Not only that, but he is also dressed in sackcloth.'

These words bewildered Esther, stunning her into silence. Her nostrils flared as she tried to breathe. The air was suddenly hot, causing her eyes to sting. She suddenly became light-headed, and quickly sat down, as her legs had started shaking. A horrible feeling of dread churned in the pit of her stomach.

'What has happened?' she whispered shakily. 'He cannot enter the city gates,' she continued in a voice that sounded hollow. Esther could not imagine what had driven Mordecai into this state, but she knew it had to be something serious. She had already suffered enough heartbreak when both of her parents died; the thought of Mordecai, the only person now left in her family, being in distress made her heart ache. After her parents' deaths he had taken her in, and his strength, care and unconditional love had helped her put her life back together again. A further wave of fear broke over her as she tried to imagine what might be going on. She dared not go to Xerxes until she knew the exact nature of this problem.

Esther's palms sweated as she thought of Mordecai sitting outside the gates in sackcloth. *He should not be seen in that state!* Her first logical thought was to have a fresh set of clothing taken to him, so she summoned one of the eunuchs and ordered him to deliver it. Deep in her heart she knew that this was not the solution, but felt she had to do something. It was not like him to put on sackcloth; he was one of the king's officials, well paid and lacking nothing. She was not sure what her uncle's response would be, but she didn't have to wait too long to find out – her heart sank even deeper when in no time at all the eunuch returned with the clothes untouched.

Esther grew increasingly agitated. She needed to know the cause of Mordecai's distress. She had an inkling that whatever was bothering him would in some way affect her as well, and a fresh chill ran down her spine. At that moment she could have had no idea of the magnitude of the problem she was about to face. Running out of options, she asked for Hathach, the eunuch assigned to attend to her. She knew it was risky to involve him because he would most likely report back to the king, but she felt that she had no other option.

'I understand that Mordecai is dressed in sackcloth and covered in ashes,' she started haltingly when he arrived.

'Yes, Your Majesty. He has been told to stay outside the city gates,' Hathach responded, uncertain whether she was aware of this fact.

'Yes, I am aware of that,' Esther responded. 'That is why I would like you to approach him and find out what has caused this behaviour.'

'I will go immediately,' he replied, honoured to be entrusted with this assignment.

It was easy for Hathach to spot Mordecai – the solitary figure standing at the gate, at a distance from the travelling crowds. He approached him with caution as he was not sure of his mental state; he looked like a madman.

'I have just been with Her Royal Majesty, Queen Esther, and she is concerned about you,' he started. The queen was highly respected by everyone in the kingdom, and Hathach mentioned her name to make sure that he had Mordecai's attention and cooperation.

'I have brought a great ordeal upon myself and my people,' Mordecai responded in a hoarse voice. Hathach stared at him with a puzzled look on his face; he was unaware of the struggle between him and Haman. Mordecai explained the whole story to him in detail, and ended by saying, 'Haman is now on a mission not only to destroy me, but also all of my people!' Mordecai fumbled in the small bag that lay beside him and pulled out a short scroll of parchment. 'He has already drawn up an edict which has been distributed to all the provinces,' he said, handing the copy over to Hathach.

'Oh!' Hathach was astounded as he read through the edict. His eyes were quick to notice the king's seal and signature.

'Please show this to the queen,' instructed Mordecai. 'Ask her to approach the king and plead for this edict to be nullified.' He then added chillingly, 'If this is not reversed, we will all perish!' Hathach suddenly realised that he was dealing with a deeply serious matter.

Esther was in great turmoil when she learned the cause of Mordecai's distress. She was even more agitated by his request. She knew it was against the law for her to go into the king's inner court without being summoned. She wondered angrily why such a draconian law had ever been made. *The king should be accessible at all times.* She pictured herself approaching the inner court and the king not extending his golden sceptre. She was filled with fear as she suddenly thought of how Vashti had been banished from the kingdom.

'Please go back and tell Mordecai that he has requested me to do the impossible,' she told Hathach. 'I cannot approach the king's inner court without the sceptre first being raised to me.' She felt defeated because she knew in her heart of hearts that her uncle already knew this, and yet he still wanted her to do it.

The response he sent back cut her to the heart: 'Esther, how do you know that you were not raised for such a time as this? If you do not rise to the occasion and help us, the effects of this threat might be worse than you can imagine, and utterly disastrous for all of us – including yourself.' Esther realised that the lives of her people were in grave danger, and that she was the one person best placed to avert this catastrophe.

'Leave me for a moment,' she told Hathach. She could well understand Mordecai's desperation, but she needed time to think. *Why isn't there a better solution than my having to go against the king's law?* she thought to herself. *I could die!* But she also knew that she would certainly die, along with all the other Jews, if Haman succeeded with his mission.

Esther's spirit was deeply troubled. She could not see a way out for her and her people. She suddenly felt forsaken, and she yearned for the sturdy guidance of Mordecai. She sat motionless on the couch, drained of all energy, and a dark cloud of fear began to creep up on her.

She rose and went to stand by the window, where she gazed out at the hills in the distance – they were standing steadfast, and were beautiful and serene, a sharp contrast to the agitation that was churning within her. She knew that although they looked smooth and green from her vantage point, in reality they were covered with rocks and thorns. She felt a shiver go down her spine as she pictured herself running up them barefoot, the sharp stones and thorns cutting into the soles of her feet. As this painful picture formed in her mind, Esther became aware that her spirit was being shown something very different – that she did not need to worry about the stones and thorns in her imagination, instead she needed to concentrate on the distant beauty and wholeness that she could see.

She could not explain it, but a peace started to rise within her, shifting the dark cloud of fear and giving her clarity about what she needed to do to save her people. She must approach the king and alert him to what was happening. She had a sense that they would be safe if she presented her case to him. She was reminded of Mordecai's ongoing instruction that she take everything to the Lord in prayer. *I will prepare myself to approach the king's inner chamber,* she decided.

Esther resolved to go into a time of intense prayer and fasting for her people. She knew the burden was too great for her to carry on her own, so she sent word to Mordecai for others in the Jewish community to fast together with her before she went into the presence of the king. They were not to eat for the three days and three nights, as they prayed for Esther to find favour with the king and in having the evil edict reversed. She was uncertain how Mordecai would respond to her request, but she felt peace within her as she settled on this course of action. She kept her eyes on what she had been told to, and pictured herself running up a hill beside a gurgling stream, beautiful flowers and soft green grass cushioning the soles of her feet. The pleasant vision made her smile as she returned to the couch and called for Hathach to communicate her decision and request to Mordecai.

Esther knew that she needed supernatural strength to accomplish the task that lay ahead of her. Not only was she planning to break protocol by approaching the king's inner chamber without being summoned, but she was also seeking to have the edict that he had signed revoked! The sharp paradox of these two actions was unmistakable, and she knew that she would need grace if she was to succeed in obtaining the favour and victory she so badly wanted. *There is no time to waste, I must do this now!* she declared to herself.

Esther knew that fasting was an act of faith, one that would strengthen her to focus on and face her task without any fear. She had fasted in the past, but this would be her first experience of doing it for much longer. Previous times of fasting had required much strength and willpower, and she wondered how she was going to last three full days and nights. Her mind found excuses as to why she should not embark on this journey, and a few chilling thoughts filled her mind. *It cannot be healthy for you, Esther; your body will shut down, and you will collapse and die!* Then she recalled how she had felt strengthened after each and every one of the fasts she had undertaken in the past, and she warmed to the idea. *I will have sufficient grace at my disposal to see me through this.*

Esther considered all the activities she had scheduled for the coming days, and wondered if she should cancel these during her fast. But this would involve breaking promises she had made, which did not feel right to her. Knowing how much all of these commitments required her input, she resolved to carry out her duties as normal during the day, and then to pray when she got back later on in the afternoon and in the evening, when she had retreated to her private chambers. It so happened that Xerxes was going to be away for the next few days, so excusing herself from the royal chambers would not be difficult.

'I will make sure that the chambermaids keep you well stocked with firewood and hot water,' Xerxes had assured her after she had informed him of her plans to go on a retreat.

'There is already enough firewood, and the water is always piping hot,' she had protested. But she knew that it was just Xerxes being Xerxes – he always wanted everything to be perfect for her!

Esther had her own suite of private chambers, which was always kept ready for her, and which provided her with a haven of solitude whenever she required it. It comprised a lounge, bedroom, bathroom and kitchen, and she had refurbished it to her own taste – so that it exuded a warm, down-to-earth and homely atmosphere.

That night, before going to sleep, Esther knelt at the foot of her bed and prayed for the coming days. She prayed that she would receive guidance and supernatural strength throughout the fast. She lifted up all the Jews who would be joining her in fasting, praying that they too would be strengthened to continue standing with her. The thought that so many others would be joining her gave her fresh courage.

21

THE FAST

ESTHER WOKE UP A little earlier than normal on the first day of her fast. As she tidied up her room she found herself singing some of the songs the Jews sang whenever they gathered together for worship. She wanted everything to be neat and tidy for when she came back from her meetings. *I might as well do this while I still have some energy,* she thought to herself. *Who knows, I might be barely crawling by the time evening arrives.* She then went on to have a bath, and was done in no time. Soon her aide came and collected her, and she set off on her busy schedule.

She was relieved to walk back into her chambers after her long day out. Everything was just as she had left it, as she had requested that housekeeping only be done at the end of her stay. She headed straight for her bedroom and threw off her shoes, replacing them with soft, comfortable slippers. She then knelt at the base of her bed and prepared to go into a long session of prayer. She had planned this all before, and was excited to be finally doing it. She knelt in silence and waited for inspiration about what exactly to pray. But her mind would not settle, and kept racing back and forth, and she found herself struggling to focus. She tried giving praise, but still she couldn't concentrate. She eventually decided to simply kneel in silence, but this too didn't seem to work, and a large knot of frustration started building up inside her. She could not understand why she was finding it so hard to pray.

The situation facing her people was formidable, yet here she was failing to make clear petitions. Frustration got the better of her and, seeing that she was not going anywhere, she ended her prayer session. With some disappointment in her heart, she decided to have a bath instead. She was dismayed that she had not been able to pray as she had wanted to. As she lay back in the warm, soapy water her mind drifted to Xerxes, and she wondered what he was doing at that moment. She knew that usually this was the time she would be giving him a rundown of her day, had it been any ordinary day. She must have then drifted off to sleep, for when her eyes next opened, the sun had already gone down and the water was no longer warm. So she hastily got out and donned her comfortable night garments.

Esther felt a bit more settled now as she sat on the couch. Her body had been craving food earlier on, but had now settled down. In the stillness she started reflecting on some of the past teachings she had found helpful. A particular passage of scripture came to mind, one which she had held on to throughout her life; it told her that her future was bright and filled with hope, and how nothing that the enemy devised against her would ultimately prosper. She closed her eyes in prayer, and this time the words flowed freely from her lips as she asked for grace for her people to be saved. The words 'I Am' kept resonating in her spirit. She could not explain it, but a fresh surge of energy coursed through her spirit as she prayed. *Thank you that you are with us, you will not leave us or forsake us; you are the I AM, and you will uphold us with your right hand; you will protect each and every one of us because you are our great help; you are the great I AM – nothing is too hard for you.* Esther eventually went to bed with a sense of peace surrounding her.

The second day dawned, and Esther said silent prayers as she lay under the covers for just a little bit longer. She was uncertain about how she was going to fare that day, and a soft voice of apprehension whispered in her mind. She silenced it by singing songs of worship in her heart. She eventually roused herself and knelt at the foot of her bed. She was thankful for this new day, and prayed for fresh grace to sustain her throughout it; this was something that she usually did at the start of each day. She then prayed for peace, love and mercy to reign everywhere. She pleaded that the weapon formed against her people would be pulled down, and every word spoken against them reversed. She prayed for favour when she made her request known to Xerxes, and asked for strength as she went about her daily tasks.

Esther was going to need supernatural energy to keep her going, as she had a packed day ahead. She planned to visit an orphanage, and then to spearhead a campaign started by a group of widows who were doing market gardening at a site the king had donated to them. Her final task was to meet with a small group of community leaders from whom she received regular updates about their designated sections. She always found these meetings interesting and informative, and was always amazed at the passion they all put into their commitments.

The time flew by, and Esther threw herself wholeheartedly into these tasks. She kept praying for strength to infuse her hungry body, and no one she met with knew that she had not had food or water for two days now. Nothing had changed in her demeanour; she remained her usual cheerful self. She politely refused all offers of meals, choosing instead to keep busy by taking a walk when the others sat down to eat.

As she rode home that evening, Esther was uncertain if she would be able to last another night; she felt weak and drained. However, the seriousness of their situation propelled her on, and she knew she had to finish her planned schedule of fasting. She was grateful for the solitude her chambers provided, and soon she was soaking in a warm, soapy bath. She lay in the water for quite some time, and when she was done she decided to take a walk in the gardens. The breeze was cool, and was just what she was need-ing at that moment.

'Thank you for the fresh breeze and your beautiful creation sur-rounding me,' she murmured, her eyes lifted towards the heavens. She was not surprised to find that she seemed to have acquired a heightened sense of smell; she could distinctly pick out the aroma of delicious steak with roast potato and onions that wafted past her as she walked. She made an effort not to think about it, and started singing softly, interceding for her people – that they be saved from an untimely demise. It was just starting to get dark when she made her way back to her private chambers. The air had become cold by now, and she pulled her shawl tightly around her shoulders, looking forward to spending the rest of the evening before her fire.

Later on, as the rest of the world turned in for the night, she tried to settle down to sleep – but to no avail. She was wide awake, and she knew that no amount of meditation would help. She felt a sense of agitation that she could not place her finger on. A fear of fainting crept into her mind, and she wondered if she had stretched her physical body over and above its limits. This was the first time she had gone for so long without eating and drinking, and she wondered how her forefathers had managed it. A fore-boding voice in her head kept trying to instil fear in her, but she pushed these fearful thoughts from her mind and concentrated on all she had to gain by going through with what she had resolved to do. It was hard to explain, but she was convinced that this fast was equipping her to overcome her fears and to fight the huge battle that lay before her. She was not going to cave in to fear; she needed to keep her focus on securing victory for her people.

Esther continued to toss and turn for a while, before deciding that she needed to do something rather than keep trying to get to sleep. She propped herself up in bed, lit her lamp and reached for the bundle of scrolls by her bedside. She randomly picked one, and then carefully untied the strings and unrolled it; the title was: *The Joy of the Lord is my Strength*. She quickly read through the entire manuscript, and then went back over it again, this time reading slowly in search of Divine revelation. And it came to her that there were areas in her life that needed to be renewed; she suddenly realised that she needed to fully surrender her life to Yahweh in order to experience the strength and joy that only *He* could give. As she prayed silently in her heart she felt streams of peace flowing into her soul. She experienced a prompting in her spirit that all was well; with that she rolled up the scroll, extinguished the lamp and lay down to sleep. When her eyes next opened, it was morning.

Esther got up at the break of day and headed straight for the lounge. She drew back the drapes that ran from wall to wall, and the morning light flooded in. Her eyes fixed on the mountains in the distance, and she started singing to herself in a hushed voice. *You sound sweeter than I do*, she thought to herself as the sound of birds chirping outside reached her ears. *But all the same I will join you in lifting up praises to our Maker.*

She then wandered back to her bedroom and knelt at the foot of her bed. She could not explain it, but this was the spot she felt drawn to whenever she prayed. At the foot of her bed lay a huge wooden chest, cushioned on the top in plush velvet, and when she knelt she would rest her hands on the soft fabric.

The peace and quiet around her stilled her thoughts, and she found herself drawn into a long prayer, full of praise and worship. She felt a soaring in her spirit that spurred her on to more prayer, and she did so with hands raised high and tears streaming down her face, her soul elevated to a whole new level. Memories of her own amazing journey flashed through her mind. She remembered their arrival in Susa as exiles, and how they had been led in safety. She had felt a protective presence surrounding them back then, and now she had that same feeling again. The memory gave her goosebumps on the backs of her arms. *I am thankful that we are going to come out of this situation unharmed. We already have the victory.* Esther continued in prayer, and as she did so she felt at peace, and confident that everything was going to be okay. She was thankful for how she had always felt cared for, provided for and surrounded by a steadfast Presence.

Esther knew she would need divine strength to make it through this day, the third and final day of her fast. Although she had no meetings scheduled, today was the day that she was planning to go uninvited into the king's inner court. She welcomed the solitude that her chambers provided, as she still felt she needed time to prepare. She spent the rest of the day alternating between reading from her scrolls and praying. When she felt like praying, she mostly would go to her bedroom and kneel at the foot of her bed, or would sometimes do so whilst walking around the lounge. All she did was pray, sing songs of praise and worship, and read messages of encouragement.

Esther's mind went back to the dream that she had had the day before, in which she had been walking for some time up a mountain path and was feeling very weary. She had suddenly heard water flowing close by and had walked through the bushes to get a closer look. There she discovered a clear, fresh stream. Feeling very hot and thirsty, she had been about to kneel and scoop some up to drink. That is when she had noticed that the water was flowing *up* the mountain rather than down. While she had been trying to understand how this could possibly be, she had awoken from her sleep.

She had lain there for quite a while, trying to figure out what it meant. The image of the water flowing uphill kept playing over and over in her mind; it spoke to her of impossible situations becoming possible. She felt settled and encouraged deep in her spirit, and renewed hope sprung from within her.

As the time for her to approach the king's chambers drew near, Esther rang for her bath to be made ready. As it was being prepared she went into her dressing room and picked out what she was going to wear under her royal robe. Thoughts crept into her mind about how Queen Vashti had been banished from the palace because she had not come when Xerxes had called her. She thought it ironic that she now was going into the king's inner chamber without being summoned. She knew that what she was planning to do went against the rules of the kingdom, and was tantamount to treason, but she was ready to face the consequences of her actions, even if it meant being banished or hanged. Esther had no fear in her at all as she made her way to the king.

<u>22</u>

THE INVITATION

THE TWO GUARDS AT the door of the inner court of the king seemed undecided on how to react as they saw the queen approaching; they had not been informed that she was coming. Esther could see that Xerxes was sitting on his royal throne, facing the entrance. A sombre atmosphere pervaded the place. Upon seeing her, the king looked up and fastened his eyes on her; she who seemed to have a reverent glow all around her. Her sudden appearance pleased him immensely, and his heart felt a renewed surge of love for his beautiful wife. He would have risen and taken her in his arms, as he had missed her intensely over the last few days, but protocol prohibited this. He was delighted she had come into the inner chamber; she was like a breath of fresh air, and provided a pleasant distraction from all his duties. After the disappointing actions of Vashti, she was the best thing that had ever happened to him, and he was thankful that everything had turned out so perfectly. He had only met her because of Vashti's disobedience, and would never have married her had Vashti not defied him.

The king was delighted to see Esther, and immediately raised his golden sceptre as a gesture for her to approach. She walked gracefully towards him, approached the throne, and touched the tip of the sceptre. Xerxes immediately knew that something was troubling his queen, and his heart ached at the thought of it. All he wanted to do was to take her troubles away and make her happy again.

'What is on your mind, my dearest Esther? Make your request known and I will make it available to you, even up to half of this kingdom.'

'If it pleases Your Majesty, I would be humbly honoured if you would attend a special dinner, I have prepared in your honour this evening.' Esther had decided to tread carefully with her request.

'Of course, my queen, I would be delighted!' Xerxes was pleased, and it showed.

'I know Haman is your trusted advisor, and I would be honoured if he would attend the dinner too,' she added.

'Are you sure there is nothing you want me to do for you before then?' he asked, sensing that she was holding back with something.

'Nothing more than your esteemed presence at dinner tonight, Your Highness,' she replied, with a sweet smile. 'Everything else will be made known in due course.'

Esther exerted herself in preparing for the coming occasion. Her guests were served tender beef steaks, baked potatoes stuffed with cream and cheese, and roasted vegetables freshly harvested from the king's garden. The meal was delicious and heart-warming. Xerxes yearned more than ever to give Esther what she wanted.

'Make your request known, dear Queen Esther, and I will grant you whatever your heart desires, even up to half of this kingdom,' he told her again.

'What my heart desires,' she replied, 'is for you and Haman to come to a banquet I will be preparing in your honour tomorrow evening. I will make my request known at this time.' She was not to be rushed.

The king tried to coax her into telling him what this request was, but she gently repeated that she would make it known only at the banquet the following day. No amount of coaxing could make her reveal it before that time. Haman, wondering what this request could be, eventually went home, leaving the king and queen to spent the rest of the evening together in front of the warm glow of the fire.

Haman was honoured and thrilled that the queen had acknowledged his position of importance in the kingdom by personally extending another invitation to him. His mind now played over the events of the evening. There had been only the king, the queen and himself seated around the royal dinner table.

Life cannot get better than this, he thought as he rode home. *Haman, son of Hammedatha, is now dining with royalty*. He was in exceedingly high spirits. He felt accomplished and perceived that he was the king's favourite officer. *Watch this space*, he boasted to himself. As the carriage approached the city gate he saw Mordecai sitting there in sackcloth, and he seethed inside. He despised Mordecai and his people, and was still filled with rage because he had not bowed down as he rode past. He got some feeling of comfort from the other nobles at the gate, as they all fell in the dust as he approached, loudly raising their voices in praise as he passed. But Mordecai did not budge; he neither acknowledged him, nor did he bow.

'Your days are numbered,' Haman muttered under his breath. He chose to restrain himself from saying anything at this stage, for he knew his plot to annihilate the Jews was fast approaching. Feeling comforted by this thought, he allowed a wicked smile to light up his face.

Haman was impatient to get home and tell everybody of his good fortune. He called together his friends and family, and began recounting how the king held him and the work he did in high regard, and how he trusted him to the extent of giving him the use of his royal signet ring. Haman boasted about his wealth and the number of sons he had, and that his position was higher than those of all the other officials and nobles. He fell just short of claiming that he was equivalent to the king.

'Queen Esther invited me to her private dinner party today,' he gloated. 'It was just me, the king and her at the table.' He basked in the admiration of his friends and family, and continued boasting. 'I am now dining with royalty,' he reiterated. The fact that Esther had invited him to her private dinner party was clear proof that his presence and input was treasured at the palace. He revelled in this success, and glowed with self-satisfaction.

A dark frown suddenly clouded Haman's face, as he recalled how Mordecai had continued to refuse to bow down to him. Bitter feelings of hatred rose within him, and he wondered how he could make this man suffer for this defiance. His wife and friends all then offered suggestions as to how he could make him pay. One suggestion pleased him the most, and he decided to act on it.

He would have a towering seventy-five-foot gallows built in the morning, and get the king to have Mordecai hanged on it; after that, he and the king would celebrate at Esther's dinner. The thought filled him with great satisfaction, and he wasted no time in having it built. Nothing like it had ever been seen in the land. Gallows were a mark of finality; no one who had been hanged on one of them had survived. He felt excited, satisfied that his problem would soon be dangling in the air. So the gallows were built with Mordecai in mind, and they stood there seventy-five feet high.

'Mordecai has bought this upon himself,' he told his family. 'All he had to do to save his own life was to bow down and honour me.' He was impatient to have this problem resolved once and for all.

Meanwhile, back at the palace, King Xerxes could not settle down to sleep. He tossed and turned, and felt an unfamiliar churning in the pit of his stomach which he could not put his finger on. No amount of meditation would allow him to sleep. He eventually got up in an ill temper and ordered that the book of the chronicles of his reign be brought in and read to him.

He listened intently as the records were read out, imagining the events as they happened and bringing them back to life in his mind. After all, he was the main character in them all. His ears pricked up when they came to the last entry in the record – about the attempt on his life by Bigtha and Teresh. He heard how Mordecai had exposed their plot and thereby saved his life. He did not recall anything special having been done to honour Mordecai for this brave and noble act. *I could have been assassinated, had it not been for Mordecai's tenacity,'* he thought. He quizzed his attendants about what honour and recognition Mordecai had received for this; they told him that nothing had been done.

'That must change,' he said, speaking more to himself than to them. 'How can such a contribution to saving the king's life go without some form of appreciation? Mordecai saved my life, so why has his bravery been overlooked?'

The king was suddenly overcome with the realisation that he owed his life to Mordecai, and decided he must bestow the highest honour upon him. But he could not decide on a fitting reward – one that would give Mordecai the recognition he deserved. *The whole kingdom needs to know that I, King Xerxes, appreciate those who stand by me, and those who save my life.*

Xerxes was still trying to decide how best to honour Mordecai when Haman walked into his courts the next morning. He made his way into the king's presence to discuss Mordecai's hanging, thinking that he would be pleased with his initiative in having the gallows built in advance. Xerxes had, unbeknownst to him, summoned Haman to help him with a dilemma relating to the very same person; he felt sure that Haman would come up with an honour befitting to Mordecai.

'What honour can be placed on the person in whom the king delights?' the king launched straight in, with much gusto. 'The one person he owes his life to? Now don't restrain yourself; I intend to hold nothing back in showing my appreciation to this person.' The king looked expectantly at Haman as he waited for his response.

Haman's heart did a little somersault in his breast; he assumed the king was referring to him! *I am that person the king delights in; he owes his success to my wisdom!* he thought. *I must make the most of this; the whole kingdom needs to witness my elevation.* An elaborate picture sprang to mind, one in which he saw royal honour being bestowed generously on him. He must ensure that that honour be known by the entire kingdom, so that they could all see just how much he was appreciated by the king. Then the ears of all he passed would tingle with his praise. The king had asked him, and he now responded with great confidence. He puffed out his chest and cleared his throat.

'Well, Your Majesty, you are the greatest king that has ever reigned, taking this kingdom from strength to strength. All of your enemies quake whenever they hear your name. You are all power-ful and mighty.' Haman was warming to the task, and would happily have gone on singing his praises, but that he noticed Xerxes had started to tap his thumb on the desk with some impatience. 'If it pleases Your Royal Highness, you could have your revered servant wear one of your royal robes and ride on one of your royal horses. One of your noble officials could then lead him around the city with pomp and fanfare, and proclaim 'This is what is done for the man the king delights to honour!" Haman was elated with his plan, picturing himself in that royal robe and being led around the city by the king's official, and being established as the centre of atten-tion for years to come.

'Excellent!' declared the king. 'This is why you are my most trusted adviser.' He was delighted with Haman's elaborate plan, and satisfied that it would ensure that Mordecai would receive the recognition he deserved.

'I do try,' responded Haman with the humblest look that he could conjure up, all the while waiting for the king to confess that *he* was that esteemed servant.

'That is such an articulate plan, and I like it!' bellowed Xerxes, clearly excited. 'Now go and fetch my favourite robe, the golden one, and have my white horse brushed and prepared to be ridden.'

'By white horse you mean your treasured Pegasus?' Haman asked for clarity, scarcely believing that Xerxes would allow this treasured horse to be ridden by anyone else.

'Yes, Pegasus,' answered Xerxes. 'I want everyone to see that I am very grateful to this person. I am trusting that this demonstration of gratitude will similarly inspire others to defend the honour of their king and kingdom too.

'I will prepare everything just as you wish, Your Majesty,' answered Haman in a voice quivering with excitement. He did not waste any time, but set off to make ready all that the king had ordered. He went to great lengths to make Pegasus look royal and grand; he had him brushed until he gleamed, and then made sure that the golden saddle and equally stunning royal-crested breast-piece were placed on him. Haman considered that only the best would do – after all, he himself would be riding Pegasus. Or so he thought.

'Everything that you requested is now ready, Your Majesty,' announced Haman.

'Excellent!' roared Xerxes. 'Now go and find Mordecai, and carry out all you have advised upon him. You are my most trusted advisor, and will therefore have the honour of leading him around the city, just as you suggested. I want people to know that good deeds are appreciated and rewarded!' Pleased that his orders were about to be carried out, Xerxes did not notice the sudden change in Haman's demeanour.

'Did you say Mordecai, Your Majesty?' Haman asked, trying to hide the tremor in his voice. He was in a state of shock, and thought that he must have heard wrong.

'Yes, Mordecai,' replied the king, unaware of the upheaval he had just caused in Haman's world. 'He deserves no less, and we should have done this sooner.'

It was as if a sharp sword had pierced Haman's heart, and a sudden rush of heat made him start sweating profusely. It was a rude awakening for him to realise that the king had had Mordecai in mind all along. He felt deep humiliation as he had never felt before, but he knew he could not defy the kings order! He, the king's most trusted advisor, was going to have to lead Mordecai around town, blowing the trumpet and heralding the very proclamation that he had created. And he had imagined it would be himself riding the horse!

The three men who had betrayed Mordecai to Haman were the first to catch wind of the turn in tide for Mordecai.

'Did you hear? Mordecai is going to be given a demi-crown,' the first declared.

'A demi-crown? For what?' queried the second, incredulously.

'For defying Haman,' responded the third, jocularly.

'I have it on good authority that Mordecai is being recognised for bringing to light a plot to assassinate the king, a deed that saved the king's life,' proclaimed the first. 'Haman is going to be blowing the trumpet and praising him for this deed to the people.'

'Well, that is going to be very embarrassing for our Haman,' the second man responded, a pained look on his face.

'Haman is falling out of grace at an alarming rate,' they all agreed. 'Now hush! Here he comes.'

Haman could not make eye contact with anyone as he approached the gate. He had a eunuch in tow, leading the horse and carrying the king's robe.

'Mordecai,' he began stiffly. 'The king would like to acknowledge the good deed you did in averting a threat to his life.' He did not wait for Mordecai to respond before continuing. 'Would you please go and clean yourself up and put on the king's robe and gold neck-chain. I will wait for you here, as I will be leading you around on his horse, proclaiming your good deed throughout the city.'

'This is what is done for the man the king delights to honour!' proclaimed Haman loudly as he led Mordecai through the city streets. Word had quickly got around, and they were lined with people waving and cheering as Mordecai passed. The entire city was delighted that the king had remembered the good deed that he had done, and they all felt proud to see one of their own being honoured by him.

Mordecai felt very humbled to be given such a public accolade. Not even in his wildest dreams could he have imagined that he would ever have an opportunity to ride this exquisite royal horse. He was deeply grateful to the king for honouring him so profoundly. He could not imagine the turmoil that Haman was going through right now; all he could see was the back of his head as he went before him blowing the trumpet.

Walking all the streets took quite some time, and Haman was not only hot, tired and humiliated at the end of it, but his voice had also gone hoarse from repeatedly proclaiming 'This is what is done to the man the king delights to honour!' He had had to repeat this every time they met a fresh crowd or turned a corner. He had wanted the ground to open up and swallow him; he wished with all his heart that he would wake up and find that this had all been a bad dream. The tables had turned on him without warning, and he did not know how he was going to put things right. He rushed back to the refuge of his home as soon as he could and recounted his humiliating ordeal to his wife and friends.

'This does not bode well for you, dear friend,' they told him straight. They doubted the king would now permit any persecution of Mordecai and the Jews. They did not mince their words, cautioning, 'You have to find a way of saving face, dearest brother! The king will not lay a finger on any of those Jews, mark our words.'

There was however, not much time to discuss this issue further, and Haman had only enough time to change out of his dusty, sweaty clothes before being whisked away by the king's eunuchs to attend Esther's dinner party.

23

THE RECKONING

ESTHER HAD GONE ALL out in preparing for the second dinner party. The table was laden with choice food, and she had chosen only the best wines to go with the meal. She quickly sensed the subtle shift in Haman's demeanour as he entered the room. Usually one to walk with a spring in his step, and always sure to make a grand entrance, he displayed none of this this time. Esther presumed that this had everything to do with the humiliation he had suffered that afternoon. She knew in her heart that the chains that had bound her people were starting to crumble, and she felt encouraged by the hope that it would all soon be over. Xerxes had also picked up on the tension in Haman, and Esther watched calmly as the king tried his best to put him at ease.

'It's just your queen and I,' he cajoled, and then tried to crack a light joke. 'Dining with us appears to have got you into a tight knot; we really need to practise this more often!'

As the meal progressed King Xerxes could not endure the suspense any longer; he needed to find out what was on Esther's mind and fulfil her request.

'Would you now make your petition and request known to the king, my dear Queen Esther? Whatever it is will be granted to you, even up to half of the kingdom.'

Esther knew the time was now ripe to make the fullness of her requests known to the king. She said a quick prayer in her heart before she responded in a clear voice, 'If I still have your favour,' she started, 'would the king please grant me my life? That is all of my petition.'

Xerxes was confused at the nature of this request, puzzled by what she could mean by it. But before he could ask her to elaborate, she added, 'And could the king also spare the lives of my people along with mine? That is all that I request.' Xerxes was even more confused; he could not for one moment fathom why anybody wanted his wife, his dear Queen Esther, dead. Why did Esther appear to be begging for her very survival?

'I have heard your request, my dearest queen, but would you care to elaborate? Where is this request coming from?' An uncomfortable feeling starting to rise within him, and he wondered if there was rumour of another assassination attempt. Esther was relieved at the king's invitation to explain further.

'An edict has been issued to execute all of my people and myself along with them,' she explained.

'What is the reason for this edict?' he asked, still not quite understanding anything. 'Did you just say that you are to be executed?' he asked incredulously.

'No, it is just the disobedient Jews who are to be executed,' chimed in Haman, not having realised that Esther was a Jew. 'They are spread far and wide throughout your kingdom, Your Majesty, and they have the potential to cause problems in the future. You must trust me on this issue; I have had personal experience in this regard. I tell you, Your Majesty, they must be stopped from rising up against us!'

'So, you know about this, do you?' questioned Xerxes, all the while keeping his eyes on Esther, for he could see that she was clearly shaken. 'Do you dare to threaten the very life of your queen?'

Suddenly confused, Haman replayed the queen's statement in his head: 'An edict has been issued to execute all of my people and myself along with them.' *No! Is Queen Esther a Jew? Why did*

I not know about this? Haman suddenly turned pale, and started sweating profusely as the seriousness of his mistake hit home. His mind started racing as he tried to find a way of controlling the damage, but his lips could form no words, and he began uttering strange croaking sounds instead. He was horrified by the sound he produced; the bewildered look on his face was as much tragic as it was comic.

'Haman, seated right here, and eating with us at this table, schemed to kill me and my people in a single day. He single-handedly planned and decreed this atrocity as an act of revenge.' Esther said calmly, turning her full gaze on him. 'I am a Jew, and all Jews are my family. He is therefore my adversary, and an enemy of my people,' she boldly added. 'Even if I were not a Jew,' she continued, 'no one deserves to die for standing up for what they believe in. Haman is both callous and cold- hearted!'

King Xerxes could not stomach all of this at once. He stood up in a fit of rage and stormed out into the garden. He could not believe that the very person he had trusted and elevated more than anyone else now wished his beloved Esther dead. His thoughts stopped for a moment, as nothing he could imagine doing to Haman could appease the anguish and anger he now felt. *How dare he threaten the life of my queen!* Xerxes' rage boiled inside him as he paced the cobbled veranda, his nostrils flaring. His eyes were stinging, and he quickly wiped them with the back of his hands.

When Haman saw the king exit in a rage he did not follow him outside as he would normally have done. Instead he stayed inside with the intention of begging the queen for forgiveness, in a bid to preserve his life. He knew the king's verdict would be to banish him, or worse.

'I take everything back!' he implored. 'I let it all get out of hand, and I take it all back! Please call the king off; I can make all of this go away,' he begged as he knelt before her. 'It was all a terrible misunderstanding; I have learnt my lesson!' he cried as a last resort as he heard the king coming back into the room. But just then he caught his feet in his long-tailed coat as he hastily tried to rise from where he was kneeling, then lost his balance and, stumbling forward, landed on Esther's lap.

'What on earth do you think you are doing, you low life?' Xerxes drew near just as Haman's head hit the queen's lap. He could not even bring himself to mouth his name. 'Have you not done enough damage already? Do you now want to molest the queen in my presence?' Xerxes was both appalled and enraged at the same time; he wanted to tear Haman apart with his bare hands. He gripped the back of Haman's shirt, as he would lift a rabbit, and hurled him away from Esther. Haman fell on his back, but was grateful to be out of the king's grip. The stone-cold look on Xerxes' face was enough to start him shaking uncontrollably.

'Do you think you can beg your way out of this?' demanded Xerxes. 'You do not even deserve to be heard!' he continued in disgust. 'I now realise how cold-hearted and self-centred you are. My biggest regret is ever having trusted you at all. How could I have been so blind?' he spat the words out, not expecting an answer.

'Come here, my love! Do you think you can ever forgive me? Why did you not come to me sooner?' Xerxes extended his hand to Esther, words not enough to express his heart right now, as he hugged her protectively.

'Guards!' he called out loudly, his arms still wrapped protectively around her. 'Seize this man and lock him away, whilst I determine what to do with him,' he ordered.

'I am so sorry, Your Majesty!' implored Haman with tears streaming down his face.

'Pride got the better of me, and I will make amends – if you will only give me a second chance.' He then tried again. 'Punish me whichever way you see fit, but please spare my life!' he begged. But he may as well have been talking to himself, as Xerxes' full attention was now on Esther.

Haman was dragged from the room with no further response from the king. The sinking feeling in his stomach was deep and tormenting. He could sense his complete demise as he saw Harbona enter the room just as he was exiting.

'Harbona!' called Xerxes, as he saw him entering the room.

'Yes, Your Majesty,' he answered.

'We have a situation that needs a swift resolution,' stated the king. 'Haman has been plotting to execute the queen and her people. What can you suggest as a fitting punishment?'

'Your Majesty, that is an easy question to answer,' responded Harbona.

'How so?' quizzed Xerxes.

'You see, Haman had a grudge against Mordecai, and just this evening he had gallows built, with the intention of hanging him on it!'

'Has he now?' responded Xerxes.

'I think it would be fitting to have Haman hanged on his own gallows,' said Harbona, quite warming to his own idea.

'Where are these gallows?' asked Xerxes with much interest.

'They are right at his house,' responded Harbona. 'He also had a grandstand constructed, so that many could witness Mordecai's hanging.'

'Well, well, well!' said Xerxes. 'Let's see how well those gallows were constructed! Let him be hanged on his own gallows indeed! And make sure that the grandstand is packed. I want everyone to witness what is done to cold-hearted and cruel people in this kingdom.'

Xerxes started feeling a huge sense of relief now that a solution had been provided so quickly and so close at hand. Esther, however, knew that the battle to save her people was not yet over.

The decree Haman had issued was still executable and, if nothing was done, would go ahead as planned. She had to convince King Xerxes to cancel the decree, and urgently!

'Your Majesty,' she started, 'The decree that Haman issued will still be enforced if nothing is done to stop it.'

'And it will be too!' responded Xerxes with a worried look on his face. 'Summon Mordecai and have him write a fresh decree rescinding Haman's order, to be delivered immediately throughout all the provinces,' he commanded Harbona.

The new decree was quickly drawn up in all the different languages, and signed and sealed with the king's signet ring. It was despatched to the all the different provinces, cancelling out the first harmful decree. Whereas the first decree spoke death, the second decreed life. King Xerxes commissioned the fastest horses and the most experienced riders to ensure that the decree reached all the provinces on time. Thereby the evil voice that had accused the Jews was silenced, and the weapon that had been raised against them did not prevail.

For the Jews, this decree was received with relief and celebration. Their evil predicament had been turned around, and they now no longer needed to protect themselves. The elders reminded the people that, as in times of old, their mourning had been turned to dancing, and they had been given beauty for ashes; where they once had worn sackcloth, they now were adorned in celebratory garments. The dark cloud of death that had been hanging over their heads had been lifted, and they could see the blue skies once again. Great celebrations could be heard everywhere the decree was delivered. There was news that some people had quickly converted to the Jewish faith because they feared for their lives, and all now worshipped Yahweh.

Days later, Mordecai left the king's presence adorned in royal garments of blue and white and a purple robe of fine linen. King

Xerxes had elevated him to second-in-command, and a large crown of gold sat on his head. Mordecai was held in high respect by all, as he had worked for the good of his people by standing up for what he believed in.

Ultimately Haman's hateful plot towards the Jews was turned on him instead, and he ended up being hanged on the very gallows that he had built for Mordecai. Not only Haman, but his ten sons too. Ironically, his estate was taken over by Esther, under the management of Mordecai, his sworn enemy and the man he loathed.

The exact days of the Jews' troubles and their eventual restoration were recorded, and Mordecai issued a command for this time to be commemorated each year from then on. Known as Purim, it became a time for remembering how they had been delivered from the jaws of death. Each year they celebrate this remembrance with song and dance, and in giving gifts to one another, and by giving alms to the poor. A fitting commemoration indeed!

24

SOLID GROUND

ESTHER SAT IN THE king's favourite spot, his chair on the north-facing balcony, overlooking the gardens. They were as beautiful as always, and today she gazed at them with a heart full of thanksgiving and praise. She could still catch a faint whiff of Xerxes' musk perfume as she leaned back into the soft cushions. She rocked herself gently back and forth, enjoying the serenity and the beauty of the scenery before her. The events of the past few days had been hectic, and she was relieved to be able to sit back and revel in the sweetness of victory. She knew that no one was going to disturb her; the king had gone out and the housekeepers had already done their rounds for the day.

The bowl that always sat beside Xerxes' chair had been replenished with freshly-picked fruit. The grapes looked tempting, and she wondered if he would playfully growl, 'Who has been eating my fruit?' or 'Who has been sitting in my chair?' when he found out she had been there. The thought of Xerxes lit up Esther's face. She loved him so very much, and she wished he were there with her at that moment. She sunk deeper into the cushions, in an attempt to take in the last vestiges of the faint perfume that still lingered there.

Esther had always known her Uncle Mordecai to be a man of faith, but at that moment, as she sat on the balcony as queen, she realised the magnitude of his faith. She had witnessed how he had held on to that very faith that had been passed down to him through the generations, and in doing so had won a great victory for his people. She recalled how she had almost despaired as she had assessed the situation with her own eyes, but now she plainly understood what the Book of the Law meant when it said, 'Our ways are not His ways,' and 'Nothing is impossible for Him'. She recalled how she had sometimes felt hopeless – because she had been trying to solve the problem in her own strength and had momentarily forgotten to give the burden to the Lord.

She had learned this great truth as she had journeyed through her fast, going for three days and three nights without any food and drink. She had felt a souring faith with each passing day and the confidence that she and her people were loved and protected. She had witnessed with her own eyes the fall of Haman and his family. This man had intended to destroy her and her people, but she had seen this injustice and evil overturned, and her people delivered.

Esther closed her eyes and worshipped deep in her heart. The Lord had been good to her; He had walked with her through her not-so-easy life. He had lifted her, raising her from foreigner to queen. And as she sat in the king's soft, warm chair, overlooking beautiful gardens, she knew it could only be her mighty Redeemer who had lifted her out of the miry clay and placed her feet on solid ground. *I am on solid ground*, she murmured to herself, tears of joy and gratitude welling up in her eyes. She sat there quietly, surrounded by a sense of peace and love. She picked at Xerxes' grapes with feelings of gratitude and contentment in her heart. She was enjoying the solitude of this moment; everything was so beautiful, and she did not want anything to spoil it. She must have drifted off into a light sleep, because when she opened her eyes the king was kneeling before her, gazing into her face.

'Now, who has been napping in my chair?' Xerxes asked playfully, as he slid in beside her and gently pulled her onto his lap.

'I missed you,' she murmured as she snuggled into his arms, her ear tuned to the rhythm of his heart.

'I missed you too, Queen Esther,' was his gentle response.

She drew closer to him, breathing in his scent and not caring to ask why he was back so early. She was just grateful he was now here together with her in their own little world. Esther loved the king, and she silently prayed for him and for the kingdom.